Sins of the Innocent

ALSO BY MIREILLE MAROKVIA

Immortelles: Memoir of a Will-o'-the-Wisp

Sins of the Innocent

A MEMOIR

Mireille Marokvia

UNBRIDLED
BOOKS

Unbridled Books
Denver, Colorado

Copyright © 2006 Mireille Marokvia

Library of Congress Cataloging-in-Publication Data
Marokvia, Mireille, 1908–
Sins of the innocent : a memoir / Mireille Marokvia.
p. cm.
ISBN-13: 978-1-932961-25-6 (alk. paper)
ISBN-10: 1-932961-25-9 (alk. paper)
1. France—History—1914–1940—Fiction.   2. World War, 1939–1945—
Germany—Fiction.   3. French—Germany—Fiction.   I. Title.
PS3563.A678S56   2006
813'.54—dc22   2006014993

1   3   5   7   9   10   8   6   4   2

Book design by SH·CV

First Printing

To the memory

of all the innocents

less lucky than we were, humbly.

I

❧

I shall call him Abel, a name that suited his fate.

Abel did not, any better than I did, discern the web that was being woven around us as the year 1939 dawned. On a frigid February night, I sat for the first time at his mother's table. She was dignified and shy—and beautiful—under her helmet of white hair and in her high-collared long black dress. She welcomed me warmly, but her large blue eyes were on him, the prodigal son. They all had eyes and ears only for Abel. There was an older brother and his wife, an older sister and her husband, and the younger brother's wife. They all were much taller and bigger than I, and they spoke a language I did not know.

Just before supper, younger brother made an entrance. Tall, gaunt, with a sallow complexion, he wore the brown uniform I had already learned to hate through Abel's hatred. With expansive gestures he took off his greatcoat and visored cap—which his wife received devoutly. Was his yellow skull shaved or bald? All I knew about the man was that he was my age, thirty.

I stared at the blood-red armband with its black swastika as the younger brother extended garrulous greetings.

Abel, turning pale, blurted out a remark that caused an uneasy silence.

But cheerful young wife, who had been out of earshot in the kitchen, was just then rushing in with supper: a vast plate of cold cuts and sausage decorated with pickles, black bread in thin slices, and a tall, slender bottle of Rhine wine, rather than beer—in my honor, older brother amiably informed me in his broken French. I smiled feebly, evoked the velvety French soups of my childhood and grew sick with longing. The meal was short and the talk loud.

As we prepared to leave, Abel had an animated talk with his mother. She was offering something he was refusing, I understood.

Later, as we walked together on the cold street, Abel explained that his mother had had a room ready for me. The apartment she shared with her younger son, his wife, and their small child was quite large.

"No! I would not let you sleep under the same roof as that . . . uniform," he exclaimed, his anger mounting. "Nobody told me that good-for-nothing had joined the SA. I beat him up years ago for running around with that rabble! They paid him with beer then for inciting brawls at political rallies. What did he do for them that they now reward him with an office position?"

Barely four months had passed since a friend of Abel's had unexpectedly visited in Paris.

The moment I had caught sight of it at the door, I had hated the man's handsome face, smiling above a pink azalea in bloom. He had come with a message: Abel's mother was sick and so destitute she had had to borrow money from him repeatedly. Abel should return to "the Motherland" and take care of things as he had done in the past. Germany was prosperous and peaceful. Yes, yes, there had been some trouble lately—the *Kristaalnacht* in November—popular reactions, and quite legitimate too, after the murder of that German official in Paris by a Jew. The government would take appropriate measures, no doubt. Of course, the friend would gladly help Abel to find a good position.

And fast too. Abel had become an art director in an advertising agency in his mother's town. I had just joined him. We were going to stay in Germany for six months. Abel had promised: six months.

"Mother looked better tonight," he said, perhaps guessing my thoughts. "But she's so courageous, one never knows."

In orderly, ponderously handsome Stuttgart, all Abel had been able to rent was a maid's room on the top floor of a neat house in the well-scrubbed suburbs. Everybody, he said, was on the lookout for a better place for us.

Our Paris atelier had had a luminous high roof made entirely of glass, a black stovepipe dizzily ascending to it. A trapeze hanging from the open rafters invited an athletic swing from the balconied bedroom onto the dining room table.

"Be brave," I told myself. "Be brave."

Instead, I took the coward's path, I became ill.

II

I entered the Sorbonne in November 1928, ten years—almost to the day—after the French and the Germans signed the armistice that ended the Great War. A country girl, intimidated as much by the swarm of students as by the solemnity of the ancient university, I would sit, with smiles of apology, on the windowsills or the dusty steps in the forever-filled auditoriums. With great difficulty I learned to fight to gain entry to the library, secretly alarmed that one of us would go through the glass partitions of the porter's cubicle.

Our silent library with its polished floors, monumental tables, and green-shaded lamps was much too small. And the books we all needed, far too few. The timid and the unlucky had little chance when they presented their requests at the small windows of morose library clerks in gray smocks. The rumor was that the library clerks took bribes from wealthy students.

There was one student, in a frayed old coat and unseemly sabots, who always got all the books he wanted. A fairy-tale character. Abandoned on some poor folks' doorstep as a baby, a smith at age fourteen, he had learned Latin and Greek from a village priest and studied toward a bachelor's degree while doing his military service. At twenty-two he knew five foreign languages and was working toward a doctorate in Egyptology.

"All is for the best in the best possible world," we said. "The face of a genius has as much magic power as a banknote."

We were the children raised under a low cloud of fear during a long war, thankful at twenty for the clear sky above our heads, our crowded university, and all things as they were.

After having been kept in boarding schools as strict as convents, I needed time to learn to be free. After two years at the university, I had managed to get only part of a master's degree. The modest dowry that I had chosen to expend on my studies nearly gone, I took a job at a suburban school. Teaching five days a week plus commuting left one day only at the university. Moreover, poems had to be written and recited in cafés and in the salons of generous poetry fanciers; dancing, swimming had to be done. A two-week vacation in Rome turned into a one-year stay. I had not for one moment tried to resist the somber and opulent charms of the ancient city. I found work dubbing films and playing small parts in the French versions of Italian movies, never dreaming of becoming an actress but enjoying playing at being one.

This was 1933. I watched Mussolini's histrionics and Black Shirts parades, amused, disdainful, and as unconcerned as I would be later on by Hitler's oratory.

I did not take politics seriously. Perhaps because my father, a teacher, had been officially reprimanded for "mixing in politics" in his hilarious articles about potholes on village streets and nettles growing around graveyard walls. Besides, when I was in my twenties it was very unbecoming for a young woman to be concerned about politics, a man's game.

*The author in the garden of the "secluded marvel within
walking distance of the Sorbonne"*

Eventually, bored with my silly jobs, I returned to Paris, and to my former lodgings, two rooms in an eighteenth-century house, a secluded marvel within walking distance from the Sorbonne, its private garden and chapel surrounded by convents and their private gardens and chapels.

I was back at the university, making believe that time had stood still. It had not. One afternoon, a mob of right-wing students tried to keep us from attending the class of a Jewish professor. Tear gas, for the first time, filled the Sorbonne's halls.

If our genius in sabots had still been around, would we have so easily dismissed the ugly incident as something in bad taste? He would have known what it all meant. But by then, he was in Egypt deciphering ancient riddles carved on the palace walls of long-dead dictators.

At the time, I was teaching full time and taking as many classes as I could in semantics, Latin, and Greek, trying to make up for so many lost study hours. No time for worrying.

The political scene offered a disquieting spectacle, but it all seemed far away, somehow not quite real. Ministers playing musical chairs against the lurid backdrop of assorted scandals that sometimes involved the lawmakers themselves, rowdy antiparliamentary leagues in uniforms of different hues bloodying the streets. Staid citizens—the patriots by tradition—boasting that they were sending their money to Switzerland and gravely weighing the benefits of the dictatorships next door.

I remember listening to them in their salons. I also remember that I called them "old fogies" and laughed at them.

The generation whose childhood had been spent under a cloud of fear refused to accept that the sky could, so soon, darken again.

In March 1935, the German dictator declared that Germany was going to rebuild its army, despite the military restrictions of the Treaty of Versailles. Anxiety seeped into our chests. France and England, at the time, were still much more powerful than Germany. What were they going to do?

They offered impotent protests. Nothing else. Our anxiety dissipated like a morning fog.

Then the horse chestnuts burst into bloom; the dizzy Parisian spring took center stage. I was on my way to a party one evening with a group of art students when one of them—I had known him in my father's classroom—whispered that this was not the kind of party I should go to. Anyway, our group was becoming too boisterous for my taste. We were passing a Russian bar. I went in and slipped behind the black marble counter. The bartender only smiled. (These were the blessed days when bartenders, policemen, concierges, and the like still knew how to smile.)

After some time I ventured to peek over the counter and stared into a handsome, tormented face, young yet lined, blue eyes smiling but veiled with melancholy.

"I am sad tonight," he said. "Come, drink vodka with me."

I did.

He spoke with a foreign accent, was whimsical, charming. I don't remember what he said.

Like most French, I was fascinated and awed by the Russians, their literature, their history, their fate. I met them daily, the taxi drivers, bartenders, musicians, waiters, and waitresses who had, in another life, been generals, grand dukes, grand duchesses, princes, and princesses. Proud, romantic, sometimes arrogant, they were the White Russians, who could laugh and cry and sing all at once.

I also knew the other Russians, the Red Russians. A friend—a model—had taken me to the studio of Lavroff, the sculptor. A man as quiet and powerful as a tree, a fervent communist, he had an unlikely obsession with Pavlova, the famous ballet dancer and idol of the White Russians. There were only sculptures of Pavlova in Lavroff's studio, in bronze, marble, and plaster.

Thin, shabby students came, drank tea and talked, and talked, and preached in bad French about the new faith that was conquering the world. Did they ignore the sculptures for the sake of a talk, a cup of tea, or a bowl of borscht?

Shortly after Pavlova died in 1931, the White Russians sponsored a gala in her memory in the Paris opera house. For one night out of a dream, Russian generals wore their uniforms and their medals, princesses and grand duchesses their grand couturiers' dresses, their tiaras and their diamonds. I watched from the upper galleries in the company of Lavroff's model and some communist students. The sculptor's bronze Pavlova stood in a place of honor in the lobby. Was Lavroff among the Red or among the White Russians that night? I never knew. What I knew was that the Russians were too enigmatic for me.

So was the handsome Russian I had met in the spring of 1935.

I avoided the Russian bar vicinity, the artists' quarter. Twice, from far away, I saw him. Twice, I fled.

Then it was spring again. Something strange happened to my landlady: overnight, almost, she conceived an uncontrollable hatred for her beautiful, quiet house. Her hapless husband decided to sell it and advised me to look for new lodgings.

In the spring of 1936, Hitler tore up another page of the Treaty of Versailles and marched into the Rhineland, the buffer zone that could have protected France and Belgium against a surprise attack. What were "we"—France and England and our allies—going to do? The fear of war cowed members of the government and of the military as much as ordinary citizens. "We" did nothing. "We" made the shadow of war fade away for another day. And once again, our world breathed with relief. Or perhaps only I did.

I was engaged in a task impossible at this time of the year: finding an inexpensive place to live in the Latin Quarter. It was taboo, I don't know why, for Sorbonne students to live on the Rive Droite, across the Seine. In order to stay on the Rive Gauche, I had to venture farther south toward the artists' quarter.

At the end of a frustrating day, I came upon a tall, rather plain building of little interest except for a sign in the downstairs office window: "Room for Rent." I went in, was shown a small, pleasant room with a balcony. I rented it.

The walls in the whole building were painted stark white, the tiled

Abel, age twelve

floors kept bare. It looked like a hospital. But it offered a vast gymnasium on the first floor where the known athletes of the day trained, I was told, a swimming pool, a sauna, and terraces on the seventh floor for sunbathing.

There was also an artists' studio, where, I discovered the very day I moved in, the handsome Russian lived. By chance we met in the hall in the afternoon. *"Bonjour,"* we said, both smiling, both ignoring that we had not seen each other in a year. We walked out of the building. He held the door for me.

"We could have supper together tonight, could not we?" he said.

"Yes," I said.

We walked to the Dôme for the traditional aperitif before dinner.

Abel was not a Russian, he was a German. Not a very good one, he joked; his father had been born in a part of the former Austria-Hungary called Slovakia. He did not like Germany, he surely did not want to live there, he said.

III

Abel rarely spoke about his youth, but when he did, it was in an incredulous, self-mocking tone as if he did not quite believe he had been such a child or adolescent.

"My mother always boasted that I could draw pictures before I could walk," he would say. And so, on his fourteenth birthday—the family had, by then, moved to Stuttgart—she took her son to a miracle man who owned a factory and begged him to turn Abel's wondrous talents into bread-winning ones. He did . . . after three years of apprenticeship in the man's office and Abel became a draftsman with a diploma and a job. After some time, though, he decided that he would rather be a pianist. He had taught himself to play on some rickety piano in a café. Sounded pretty good, he thought. "First, I had a cutaway made to order. That's what pianists wear don't they?"

One day, in his smart outfit, his cardboard suitcase in hand, he took the train for Dresden, was accepted into the best music school in the world, and got a job in a factory as a draftsman. Real engineers were scarce in Germany in 1919. He played the piano six hours a day—his landlords loved music—and, for some eight hours, designed melting ovens. Mostly melting ovens. "My landlady delivered a giant pot of soup daily, meat on Sunday," he said. "After only a few months, the

Abel's dance band, ca. 1923

school gave me a scholarship for musical composition, and the factory entrusted me with bigger projects. A glorious life! Lasted about two years—until the day a brave bishop, in order to bless a factory I had designed, climbed on its smart, rounded roof, and ominous smoke rose from under his robes . . . the bishop's shoes were catching fire. . . .

"But by then, I had become a pianist!" Abel played to accompany silent movies, eventually returned to Stuttgart, and with three friends, formed a combo that played in nightclubs. "When I got tired of never seeing the light of day, I presented myself as an artist at the best advertising agency in town. I had only a dozen or so pocket-sized cartoons to show for myself, but I was hired." He switched to drawing and painting, even had a one-man show in a good gallery. He sold nothing, but one painting was stolen, which he found most gratifying.

Eventually, Abel got tired of advertising and one day left for Italy "in search of real art and real sun," he said. When he returned, after nearly two years, the Nazi movement, which he had predicted would go away like an ugly boil, had instead grown alarmingly. Abel had little interest in or understanding of politics, but he had strong feelings about it. He hated what was happening in Germany and saw only one solution: to run away. And so in the fall of 1928, he went to Paris to study art.

A bel had been thirteen when the First World War started, seventeen when his country lost it. He was the fifth child in a family of six. The father had died. And he had seen his mother embroidering by the light of the moon.

About the time Abel took the train for the music school of Dresden, Germans needed a bucket of banknotes to buy a stamp.

Why did he omit that somber, dramatic backdrop from the story of his youth? I wondered as I sat at the terrace of the Dôme with Abel and his friends. And indeed, he sat there every afternoon, went to a restaurant for a leisurely supper and frequently to a party. He swam, danced, camped. He painted too. On Sundays mostly, he said.

When I met him, Abel was putting the last touches to the large portrait of a woman in a romantic long black dress. Oh, how I wished he would paint me in a long black dress! Instead, he asked me to put on some Oriental blouse richly embroidered in gold, plunked an enormous hat on my head, and told me to stand still.

He painted slowly, smoked, did not talk.

I have forgotten how long it took to complete the painting, but I

Woman in Black Dress, *ca. 1935 (oil)*

have not forgotten how unhappy I was with it. I disliked the artificial forest in the background, the silly white apron I gathered in one hand, the egg I held in the other. . . . This was a fancy country girl, not me! Well, the face, the hair, the hands were mine.

"Her arm is too long," I said.

"True," Abel said. "Can't you see, there will never be enough of that beautiful blouse."

I have, at times, turned this painting against the wall. Rolled up and unprotected, it gathered dust in my parents' attic for over twenty years after we left France for the last time. And yet a day came when we clung to it as one clings to a last token saved from a shipwreck, this last image of the long-gone, happy days.

At the time it was painted I wondered whether painting was not just another luxurious hobby for Abel, like music and dance. His impromptu dancing at artistic shows made the newspapers more often than his paintings. He had once carried offstage the popular singer Marie Dubas and replaced her performance with his own extravagant dance.

Handsome, built like a ballet dancer, chic in pants on which he wiped his paintbrushes, witty, generous, and very popular, he gave the impression of not being serious about anything.

But there was a secret Abel, well organized, hardworking, responsible. His mother regularly received payments for the whimsical illustrated articles he contributed to a sports magazine published in Berlin.

His own "daily bread," as he called it, was assured by work he did for a Parisian advertising agency with which he had a long-standing gentleman's agreement—not quite legal: foreigners were permitted to do freelance work only. He was paid a regular salary and given generous vacations in exchange for whatever work fitting his talent the agency required. A boon for Abel, who usually executed a week's work in two days.

I V

When I was a child, my great-grandfather, after a long absence, returned home one Mardi Gras night wearing two similar masks, one on his face, the other on the back of his head, his wooden clogs pointing in both directions, forward and backward. Abel was just that improbable and intriguing. I was, at twenty-five, as fascinated by him as I had been by my mysterious ancestor when I was ten.

Both were men who had refused to submit to their lot but dared to follow a dream. So unlike the timorous, tedious men I had grown up with, uncles, cousins, schoolmates—even my beloved father tied, all of them, to a job or a place even when they were made miserable by it.

Abel had all their qualities, besides his exotic charm, dazzling talents and the ability to turn everyday life into a disinterested adventure.

Our backgrounds and interests were so far apart that Abel and I had almost nothing to talk about. But he was the partner who could turn me into a good dancer. We danced . . . we danced.

Abel was a doer, not a talker. Had always been, he said. "In school, I covered the blackboard with drawings: raging dragons, charging soldiers, erupting volcanoes . . . whatever came to my mind. Stopped the snickering my speech defect caused among my schoolmates."

Abel's love letters, slipped under my door almost daily, consisted of spirited sketches and cartoons and sparse, tender, witty comments. The quasi-mute messages filled me with wonder, delight, and pride.

I didn't have much in common with his friends. They were the Bohemians, poor and free. I was the bourgeois holding a job and studying semantics. My seven-year-old pupils saved me by turning out Chagalls, Monets, and Picassos that the Parisian artists snatched away. Some were avid collectors of children's paintings.

I easily abandoned the group of tormented young poets I had joined for the uninhibited artists. Forgotten, the endless discussions that had led nowhere and the wistful hours spent listening to the ancient paragon Alcanter de Brahms reading his well-constructed alexandrines out of a book bound in red Moroccan leather.

"Write a sonnet!" he had admonished when I had presented my best *"poeme en prose."*

In March, Hitler, undisturbed, occupied the Rhineland.

"When are they going to stop him?" Abel asked.

But "they," England and France, quarreled, did nothing. Most of us were relieved at that. Then April came. Braziers and glass windbreakers disappeared from café terraces, pyramids of apples surged onto the vendors' carts. In the Luxembourg Gardens, horse chestnuts lighted up a thousand candelabras of flowers. Time had come to plan the summer vacations.

"We could crisscross Spain on horseback," Abel said.

Of course we could. We started to study Spanish.

. . .

On the thirteenth of July, a Friday, Abel departed. He would buy the horses; I would join him when school was over at the beginning of August. Artists and models gave Abel a great send-off banquet complete with speeches and admonitions. At 11 P.M., we put him on the train at the Gare d'Orsay.

Our boisterous group walked back to Montparnasse. We passed Pont Alexandre. An exalted painter climbed one of the ornamented lampposts. "Abel's spirits have remained among us," he proclaimed as he came down. He then climbed the facade of apartment buildings on Boulevard Saint Germain and finally came crashing down with the neon lighting of our favorite nightclub. He disappeared into the police station between two officers only to walk out one hour later, all smiles. "A votre age, Monsieur" ("At your age, sir"), the police chief had said a bit sadly as he released him.

Ah, the Paris policemen of the '30s! They monitored traffic to let the artists' horrendous parades proceed through the whole city. They watched with us when we burned the giant papier-mâché effigy of a bad professor on Place de la Sorbonne. And the day a dozen of us student girls, decided that the waist had to go back to its rightful place and marched down Boulevard Saint Michel, our waists cinched by wide black patent-leather belts, the policemen stopped cars and trolleys.

When did those amiable policemen, together with the good days, depart?

Less than a week after Abel's departure, the Spanish Civil War exploded, and even if, at first, everyone I knew refused to take it seriously, I was in shock. I went through the last days of school like a sleepwalker. Then one cheerful letter from Abel arrived, dated July 15, confirming

Abel in Paris, 1928

our date on August 4 at 10 A.M. in front of the post office in Vigo, Spain. Against all logic—the letter had been written before the troubles had begun—I regained confidence.

Spanish consulates and banks closed, the peseta lost all value, train tickets for Spain were no longer sold.

"Vigo is a harbor. Why don't you take a boat?" a friend said.

Why not, indeed? I spent one whole Thursday rushing from one maritime company to another. Against all expectations, I found a British ocean liner bound for Buenos Aires scheduled to make a stop in Vigo on August 4. Such an incredible stroke of luck! Refused a ticket for Vigo, I bought one for Lisbon, the next port of call, imagining myself getting off in Vigo and staying there. . . . Surely Abel would approve of my adventurous spirit.

Abel, 1935

I have forgotten the name of the ocean liner I embarked on that beautiful August 1, 1936.

I was taking with me little more than an overnight bag and traveling third class—rough wooden bunk beds in tiny doorless cabins, straw sacks for mattresses, no sheets, just one gray blanket. In the narrow, dark eating area, one long wooden table and two benches were bolted to the floor. The passengers ate out of tin plates with tin forks and spoons, a food that I have mercifully forgotten.

But then, in third class there were mostly lively French, Portuguese, and German students who quickly befriended me.

There was a fourth class on the British boat, a small triangular deck at the stern where several Polish families bound for South America camped in the open. At mealtimes, the women got busy cooking food on little charcoal stoves. The rest of the time, men, women, and children huddled in one big heap and sometimes sang low, sad songs.

Second-class-passenger ladies—long dresses of pale blues and yellows and voluminous hats—often stood on their balcony-like deck looking at the third- and fourth-class decks beneath them.

First class was way up out of sight. I ascended to it, in the company of a student girl who spoke English, to consult the captain about a rumor that an ongoing battle in Vigo would prevent our boat from stopping there as scheduled.

We saw chandeliers and Oriental rugs in first class. The captain was young, and his manners were refined. On his orders, coffee was served to us, poured out of a silver vessel into cups of fine china. Alas, the captain confirmed the rumors.

But on the third day at sea, the victorious Franco commandant telegraphed our British captain that he had won the battle and pacified the city, and that British visitors were welcomed.

I was standing on deck after supper when I heard the good news and jumped for joy. My foot hit the moving deck and began to swell alarmingly. The unsmiling gray-haired nurse on board—there was no doctor—tightly bandaged my foot and leg up to my knee. "No walking," she shouted. I could understand that much. When a passenger I had befriended explained to the nurse that I had to get out in Vigo, where I had a date, the nurse, deaf to my protestations, locked me in the infirmary.

At dawn, our boat entered the beautiful deep bay of Vigo. I

watched from the porthole, which, I discovered, was located above a deck. There was a pile of cordage right under it. My luck! I squeezed through the porthole, tumbled down on the cordage. The deck was deserted except for one young man who was taking photographs. He helped me to my cabin. A few hours later, carried by two Spanish-speaking students who knew my story, I was on Spanish soil.

At 10:15 we stood in front of the post office. Abel did not show up.

We went to the military commandant, who received us as he was being shaved. The white towel tied around his neck could cover neither the array of medals and decorations adorning his broad chest nor the knives and guns strapped to his ample girth.

We inquired about a German artist who, the stamp on his letter attested, had been in Vigo two weeks before. "Is he a Russian?" the commandant asked.

"No, no, *alemán, alemán.*"

"We have only Russian spies here, and they are in jail," the commandant declared with ferocious glee.

We were dismissed.

We wandered through dead streets. Restaurants and shops boarded up, piles of rubble, an old civilian or two, truckloads of stern young soldiers wearing blood-red berets. At a makeshift place we ate fresh sardines fried in smelly oil. Downtown we passed somber walls of medieval thickness pierced with tiny barred openings. "The jail!" my companions snickered.

It did not enter my mind that Abel could be there. But he was. Jailed as a Russian spy, I would learn weeks later when his letters caught up with me in Lisbon.

He spent two appalling weeks in the Vigo jail until the answer to a telegram of inquiry sent by the German consul confirmed that, indeed, his family resided in Germany and that he had been born there.

After appropriating all his money—for room and board—the commandant ordered Abel put on a German boat and delivered to the Gestapo in Hamburg. After three days in a German jail, he was permitted to contact an artist friend who had retired in Hamburg. The friend vouched for Abel, took him to his home, and promptly sent him back to Paris.

Penniless, a ghost of his old self, Abel sat at the terrace of the Dôme in the lonesome Paris of August.

A smiling waiter brought him a week-old newspaper that had already published Abel's obituary. The manager offered congratulations and a drink. Then a young artist friend, on his way to a vacation at the seashore with his family, spotted him and took him along.

By the time I returned from Portugal in September, Abel had recovered his good looks, but he had not gotten over his Spanish ordeal. His brief talk with the military commandant, to whom he had freely presented himself, still tormented him.

"What are you doing here?" the commandant had suddenly thundered.

"Tourist."

"No más?"

"No más!"

"You are a Russian spy!"

A joke, surely, Abel had laughed.

"Alemán, alemán," he had said pointing at the passport he had just handed to the commandant.

"German passport made in Paris . . . ah, ah . . . false passport! Paris . . . communist!"

The commandant had whistled. Two soldiers had appeared, frisked Abel brutally. Minutes later, his arms up in the air, bayonets in his back, he had been marched across town in the noonday sun and thrown into the dismal, overcrowded jail. On July 21, his birthday.

This photograph was the parting gift from
Abel's co-prisoner who was led out to be shot
(Vigo, Spain, July 1936)

The inmates, all political prisoners, slept on the vermin-infested stone floor, got two sardines a day for food. The jailer was an old one-eyed murderer. Abel made his portrait—a profile in pencil on a piece of brown paper—and got in payment one glass of red wine and one cigarette a day.

Twice a week, at midnight, by the light of a kerosene lantern, a low-ranking officer read the names of a dozen prisoners designated to be led out and shot.

Abel had brought back two souvenirs: the snapshot of a tall young man and an empty matchbox, each given to him one midnight, and with their last embraces, by two fellow prisoners who were being led out.

V

~~❧~~

"But we are in Paris now, safe," I said. "Nothing has changed in our own lives. Nothing."

I taught as before but took only one course at the university. Abel worked for long hours on large, tragic canvases that people looked away from. One of these, a prison yard, I remember well. In the foreground, crouching on bare ground, a young man in a gray-blue tunic—a quasi-medieval figure—turned unseeing white eyes toward an invisible sky. In the background—memory, nightmare, or actual scene—three men squatting on straw under a dead tree mourned the naked cadaver stretched at their feet. Right behind, dangling from a makeshift gallows, two bare bodies—one did not seem quite lifeless. Beyond it all, a sunny high wall, and peeping over it a pink rooftop.

We made a brave attempt at resuming normal life. We met our friends in the cafés, went to parties, gave parties. We did not dare to say it aloud, but yes, we knew a blight had attacked the mood of our city that neither laughter nor wine could chase away. A sure sign of it was our policemen, posted at every street corner, becoming forever suspicious. Their dark glares followed us as we walked our beloved streets, sat at the terraces of our favored cafés and under the trees of our beau-

Memories of the Spanish Civil War, 1936 *(oil)*

tiful parks. As if the madness of the Spanish Civil War had spilled over our borders.

One April afternoon, the historic Basque town of Guérnica, so close to our border, was reduced to rubble by German planes. Could this be true? Newspapers had often lied. Weeks later, eyewitnesses confirmed the bombing, but by then we had already pushed the news away as if it had been only a nightmare. By summer, when Picasso's *Guérnica* appeared, we debated fiercely over the artistic merits of the painting. Only the painting.

One day a letter came from a friend of Abel's who had, a few years before, emigrated to Argentina to join an uncle who owned a factory there.

"Europe is heading for trouble," the friend wrote. "I urge you to follow in my footsteps." And he had enclosed with his letter a one-way boat ticket for Buenos Aires.

We had been sunning ourselves on the terrace of our hotel when Abel opened the letter. We did not speak for a long time.

One ticket, I was thinking, only one ticket. I would have gone to Buenos Aires with Abel. I would have gone to the end of the world with him.

"Which language do they speak in Argentina?" Abel suddenly asked.

"Spanish."

"I am not going to a Spanish-speaking country."

He held up the ticket.

"We are going to drink it," he said.

He sold the ticket. We invited friends. Our spirits were restored. "Let's go to Greece," I said.

At the beginning of August, with five other artists, we boarded old *Andros* in Marseille. We slept on deck, we lived on deck. The Mediterranean sky was sending down dozens of shooting stars that summer, and one night, sailing through the Straits of Messina, we saw Mount Etna sending back up big, fiery bunches of them.

In Athens, after our group dispersed, Abel and I decided to cross

At the Dôme, Paris, ca. 1935

the Peloponnese on foot. For days we walked through a nearly treeless landscape, under a cloudless sky, at the pace our donkey dictated, led by a guide who spoke classical Greek and knew where the gods had concealed rare trickles of clear, cold water.

Night after night, we slept under a sumptuous, infinite sky. We dreamed of walking around the world together and came to believe we could. Eastward. We would go eastward, Marco Polo's route.

Back in Athens, we made inquiries about visas at the Turkish consulate. A French passport and a German passport? Dark glares and shaking heads. We shrugged; ah, these ever-friendly Turks! Never mind, we needed more time anyway. We went on with our great voyage, sailing from one quiet, white island to another on shabby, romantic

Greek vessels. We slept, sometimes on the sands of deserted beaches, close to blue waters as quiet as a lake's, and sometimes under the broken marble columns and altars in the temples of long-abandoned gods. Travelers were sacred in ancient Greece. This did not seemed to have changed at all; we encountered only quiet courtesy everywhere. There were perhaps only half-a-dozen French painters visiting Greece in the summer of 1937. We did not meet any other foreigners.

During the trip back, the *Andros*—an ancient British passenger boat sailing under the Greek flag—got tossed badly in a sudden, violent squall that sent cooking pots and deck chairs flying overboard. We held on to the mast, scared, soaked, delighted like children by that moment of danger.

VI

꘏꙼꙼

We returned to a Paris where gloom had tarnished the gold of autumn leaves. Our cafés were nearly deserted; most foreign artists were absent, and many French artists, donning ties and coats, had wandered to bourgeois cafés. Policemen were unfriendly, people moody. Everybody blamed the Spaniards still at war, the new suave prime minister and the one who had just fallen, the dictators strutting at our borders, and, of course, "*les Anglais.*"

I went back to teaching and began cross-country running in the woods—a new addiction. Abel went back to painting and making advertising posters. We moved to a new artist's studio we loved, which was within walking distance of the Dôme, our favorite café. We gave a party. Did our best to forget the world.

For Christmas, we would go skiing in Germany. It happened that one of Abel's brothers-in-law had come upon a beautiful, unspoiled, easily accessible place. He would secure room and board for us.

On our way, we stayed overnight in stately Stuttgart, beautiful under the snow. Christmas trees, songs—well sung—delicious pastries, good German wines—a surprise—stylish traffic policemen surrounded by heaps of festive offerings from grateful citizens. I wanted Abel to share my enthusiasm. He shrugged.

Paris atelier, ca. 1937

A train filled with skiers took us up mountains that looked more accessible than the Alps. I liked that too.

We got off at a tiny railroad station. There was a one-hour walk along a pleasant, winding mountain road. Gentle slopes, evergreen trees, a few neat, solid houses. Everything clean, orderly, reassuring, as if the whole landscape had been rearranged to accommodate the people.

At a turn in the road, Abel suddenly threw his rucksack down into the snow and gestured angrily toward the valley that opened in front of us. At the bottom, a lone, elongated wooden structure crouched under a fluttering giant blood-red flag bearing the black swastika.

"I am not going to sleep under that rag," Abel said, picking up his rucksack and starting to walk back. I followed grudgingly.

At the unattended railroad station, a poster indicated that there would be only one late train.

Winter 1937

I promised I would get very sick if the place turned out to be unpleasant, and we slowly retraced our steps.

"The place" was a military training camp equipped to take in guests who did not mind rustic accommodations.

We were out skiing the whole day long. In the evening, we sometimes saw clean-shaven, heel-clicking young soldiers. The officer in charge, young, clean-shaven, heel-clicking, graciously offered us his room, a low-ceilinged affair furnished with two narrow, hard bunks. We ate the evening meal—black bread, sausage, and beer—with him and two other skiers, teachers eager to practice their French. They taught me some German.

On the last evening, as we had a glass of wine, the young officer, keen on physiognomy, analyzed Abel's features. His forehead, he said, was *"sehr gut,"* *"sehr Deutsch."* I understood that. His eyes were *"sehr gut,"* *"sehr Deutsch."* But the two lines on each side of his mouth indicated *"Polnische grausamkeit,"* he said.

Abel translated: "Polish cruelty."

I giggled. . . .

The officer turned red.

"Why Polish?" we asked.

"The name."

"It's Slovak, not Polish," Abel said.

The German officer was triumphant: *"Ja. Ja. Slavische grausamkeit!"*

We laughed about that exchange. Ah, we laughed about so many things.

VII

❧

I came back from our vacation with good feelings toward orderly, clean, comfortable Germany. The Germans, I said, were perhaps a bit clumsy, but they were so polite.

Abel was not listening.

"My friend from Argentina was right," he said. "We are heading for trouble."

The next day, he visited South American consulates. I reluctantly went along. Lines were long at the Brazilian, Argentinean, and Chilean consulates.

I inquired about a teaching position at the French school of Montevideo in Paraguay. There was a two-year wait. Good. I did not want to leave Paris.

Abel wrote several letters to his friend in Argentina. No answer came.

In March 1938, Hitler conquered Austria without firing a shot. No one budged. It was as if we had begun to think he had the right to do what he was doing. After all, Austria was a German-speaking country.

Shortly after, the editors of the Berlin sports magazine wrote that they could not continue publishing Abel's articles since he was not a member of the National Socialist Party. Help for Abel's mother was cut off. This was cause for worry.

The spring and early-summer months were a little sad. Our old cafés, the Dôme, the Coupole, were deserted, and we felt lost in the new ones that, for some reason, everyone we knew favored now. The number of our friends had dwindled. Why? Abel had recently received high praise for his painting from no less than Waldemar George, the best art critic in Paris. We fought unpleasant thoughts. The most enjoyable, at the moment, was our beautiful atelier. But then news came that the owner would want it back at the end of the year.

We spent a quiet summer in a remote village by the sea in northern Brittany. The flat, monochromatic landscape, the rare wind-dwarfed trees, the lonely little houses bewilderingly alike, the great violent waves crashing on the deserted beaches, the sullen inhabitants faithful to their ancient language all inspired Abel. He sketched the little gray-white houses and the crooked trees, green-eyed, unsmiling little girls, young boys in red pants like their fishermen fathers, farmers in their fields, the stunning tall, two-tiered granite crosses and the many granite statues—saints or pilgrims—gathered at their bases. Shortly before our departure, Abel sketched a lone, distraught woman stalking the wild beach. Back in his studio, he made a large painting of this disquieting gray figure, called it *Quo Vadis*. It turned out to be the last of the paintings from the happy days.

At the end of August, we hiked across Brittany. And then, since he had to report at the advertising agency in early September, Abel took the train home. I decided to walk the 250 kilometers back to Paris.

I chose a quiet route along the slow-flowing River Loire. It led close to famous chateaus I had always wanted to see, through orchards and vineyards where I rested on warm afternoons and ancient cities I knew only from history books. Every one of them offered a quaint historic hotel, a fine historic restaurant, a shady historic park, and everywhere

The castle at Chinon (postcard)

the lazy September air was dizzy with the scent of roses and ripening pears.

I walked between twenty-five and forty kilometers a day at a steady pace. Once, only once, I accepted a ride when my sandal strap broke. That day I arrived in Chinon at twilight. The ancient city called back memories of legend, and history that mimicked legend: Gargantua and Jeanne d'Arc.

At the Auberge de Gargantua, where I stayed overnight, the high ceilings could have accommodated a giant, and the dining table of dark, carved wood dwarfed the guests. The bed I slept in, piled up with mattresses of different thicknesses, was nearly a meter high. Above it, a lofty canopy supported by slender columns had cretonne curtains, their faded prints still showing impossibly big fruits and flowers.

The majestic ruins of the castle where, in 1433, Charles VII received Jeanne d'Arc were still there upon the hill. And so were parts of the city's medieval ramparts and narrow streets, their cobblestones not yet worn out.

Close to the Auberge de Gargantua were a few shops. In early morning, I hobbled to one that had dangling from a rusty rod above its door a metal sign with a dainty pink lady's shoe painted on it.

I climbed two high stone steps and entered an incredibly small shop. A pale young man, a ragged magpie perched on his left shoulder, sat behind a high, narrow counter. Right above his head, a lush climbing plant with bell-shaped blue flowers nearly covered a small window.

The young cobbler sang an ancient song as he leisurely repaired my sandal. I sat meanwhile on a box propped against the open door. The magpie jumped down onto the counter when I put a few coins on it. The cobbler smiled and wished me good luck.

I had a long hike before me. Tours, my goal, was forty-five kilometers away, forty of them through a dense forest.

The narrow, unswerving road of yellow gravel cut through the dark mass of the trees like a shaft of light. This was not the main road to Tours but the shortest. And a deserted one, I found. For most of the long day, no one passed by.

After hours of solitary walking, eyes riveted on trees—armies of trees, bent on erasing the puny road—I began to feel uneasy. I sat briefly at the edge of the dark woods, had a snack quite unlike the previous day's big lunch in a tranquil vineyard, and soon was marching again.

It was while crossing this forest on horseback with his escort of chevaliers in armor that King Charles VI had become insane. On a very hot summer afternoon, not a cool September day, and more than five centuries ago, at a time when bandits lurked behind every tree, I reflected, smiling at myself.

Still, the afternoon hours were oppressive, and I rejoiced when the road started to climb a hill and, at last, a vehicle passed by. A van and a

Last solitary walk, September 1938

trailer hooked to it. Both painted green, with little shuttered windows like the horse-drawn gypsy wagons of old. The odd convoy was struggling up the hill when the trailer started rolling back. Acrobat-like shadows jumped out, grabbed rocks from the roadside, blocked the wheels, rehooked the trailer to the van. The image out of a child's dream vanished over the top of the hill, the last image from the world I knew before it sank into confusion and fear.

I reached Tours in late afternoon, spent the night there, remember none of it. The 1914 nightmare resurrected the next day, September 24, 1938, has erased all recollections except one—a white poster on a gray stone wall with two oversized black words at its top: *Mobilisation Génèrale.*

"*Mobilisation générale* means war," my father had said when I was six years old. And it had come true, then.

In panic, I boarded the first train for Paris, a maddeningly slow train. At every stop I saw them again, invading my compartment, the soldiers of 1914 in soiled "horizon blue" singing "*La Madelon*," pouring red wine into tin cups.

Of the days that followed, I remember mostly the tense quiet on the streets of Paris and the anxieties we shared, Abel and I, but did not talk about. What had been done with German civilians living in France during the last war? Interned, I vaguely remembered. How? Where?

At the singularly quiet terrace of the Dôme, older artists ventured halfhearted jokes. Chamberlain was meeting Hitler, we heard. "The umbrella against the sword, the duel of the century!" someone exclaimed. Not many of us laughed. There was too much fear in the air.

At last, on September 30, France and England signed an agreement with Germany: the Munich Agreement.

No war. There would be no war. That was all we saw. And Czechoslovakia? Sacrificed. Yes, yes, but peace, we had "won" peace!

Jubilant crowds greeted Edouard Daladier, the French premier, upon his return from Munich. Grateful farmers at the border with Germany gave farewell parties for our soldiers and loaded them up with presents. A returning friend knocked on our door one night. In his military backpack he carried a freshly slaughtered goose and a bottle of Alsatian liquor.

We had a victory banquet. We had several victory banquets.

Less than two months later, Abel's German friend unexpectedly showed up. How I disliked him! I still do. After that, things went fast. On the last day of December, Abel left for Stuttgart. To this day, I remember how pale his face was when we put him on the train at the Gare de l'Est, a few friends and I.

In February, I followed him, leaving gray Paris for Stuttgart, where the air was clear, dry, cold, and invigorating, where big people looked strong and healthy and I, at once, became ill.

VIII

I didn't stay long in Abel's dismal little room. On the third day, as happens only in happy stories, a handsome couple appeared and whisked me away to their beautiful dwelling. Soon I was lying in bed in a lovely sunny room. An intriguing young woman attended to my needs. Slim in a high-necked embroidered blouse of the same blue as her eyes and black satin slacks, she moved like a dancer while her face kept the serenity of a nun's. Her name was Christine.

Christine and I communicated, with some difficulty, in her scanty French and my scantier German. Her greetings, which Abel translated, had confused me. I would never forget them.

"Congratulations! It is indeed appropriate to get sick when taking the first step on German soil."

Christine took me to her doctor, Dr. Müller, a short, small man with a square head and a knowing, forgiving smile.

"Acids, acids," Dr. Müller diagnosed.

He prescribed a strong solution of sodium bicarbonate (two pints of it daily), herb teas, enemas, and, most important, *Hunger Kur*, a draconian diet of strained mush, a bit of yogurt or grapefruit every third day.

Christine was taking notes. Suddenly she got into an argument with the doctor about Hitler and Czechoslovakia, I understood. Christine's voice rose, sarcastic and angry. Dr. Müller, a man who knew that he knew best, remained calm and smiling.

"Because he made a vegetarian out of Hitler ten years ago, Dr. Müller thinks Hitler can do no wrong," Christine scoffed as we left. "An ass in politics, but a good doctor. He will cure you."

Which did not happen as fast as expected. For weeks, I remained extremely weak, plagued by pains in the abdomen and nightmares that made me scream in my sleep. And daydreams. Always the same ones: I was going back to Paris. A friend had told me before I departed, "Come back to us if you don't like it. Don't feel stupidly ashamed." I wanted to go back. Something was telling me to go back. But I could not leave Abel.

In the end, Dr. Müller's *Hunger Kur* worked, or perhaps it was Christine's smiling and often unsmiling ministrations, or the feeling that I had been long enough a guest-patient in Christine's restless household. It included the husband, a businessman, middle-aged, good-looking, well dressed, and a bit vain, who prudently took off his party badge before stepping over the threshold of his home, a maid, who proudly displayed hers pinned onto her snow-white uniform, and pugnacious Christine, who never missed an opportunity to heap sarcasm over every one of the party's actions.

Abel visited often and stayed for dinner. Christine treated him kindly and openly showed that she felt sorry for him. She would not explain why.

During my illness, Abel's family had searched and finally found an apartment for us. Not wanting the regular cumbersome furniture available, Abel had a few pieces made to order. "And no chair," he declared. "A chair is for those who want to settle down." No chair. He would sit on a crate. He ordered a drawing table, two sofa beds, a small square table with a corner bench, and two tiny cabinets.

Abel's mother shook her head, smiled, and told me Abel had always been a bit of an eccentric. Christine helped me pick out a few cheap kitchen utensils.

In April, we moved to our pleasant but sparsely furnished three-room apartment. Located on the top floor of a three-story house in the hilly suburbs where neat, solid houses were surrounded by gardens, orchards, and tiny vineyards, it had a fine view of the city in the valley below.

Everything was well organized and practical. There was a laundry room in the basement. The tenants took turns using it. They also stoked the coal furnace in winter and cared for their share of the English garden that surrounded the house.

Six months of life in Germany was not going to be the ordeal I had imagined. Why had I been so fearful? Good order, I told myself, was a protection.

And now family, position, society demanded that Abel and I get married. Yes. Yes, we had intended to; more practical for traveling.

We got angry and upset right away: a new law required proof that our forebears had been non-Jewish for four generations. What kind of nonsense was that? But we submitted. My father and grandmother procured baptism certificates from parish priests. Abel got his own certification. And one gray morning in May, we walked down to City Hall. I did not wear the white suit and elegant hat made in Paris but a plain black suit and a hat I had concocted out of two old ones.

We met our witnesses at City Hall's door, Abel's older brother and the friend who had persuaded him to return to the Motherland.

We stood in front of a high, narrow desk draped in the Nazi flag. I listened to words I did not understand, spoken by a man I could not

Wedding, Stuttgart, May 23, 1939

see, said *"Ja"* at the right moment, probably. Abel was ceremoniously given a thick black book, *Mein Kampf*, and we were done.

We invited our witnesses for a glass of white wine in a nearby restaurant. We were served white radishes with the wine, I remember.

The festivities were over.

IX

"Yugoslavia," Abel said. "We could afford a short trip to Yugoslavia. We need fresh air."

I was ready to go.

We inquired about visas, passports, and were handed forms to fill out.

This was when I discovered that I had acquired German nationality. I don't know why I had not thought of that before. The next day, I rushed alone and in alarm to the French consul.

"If you did not declare before me, on the day of your marriage, that you wished to abandon your nationality, according to French law, you are still French," the consul said.

"I want to make a declaration that I wish to keep my French nationality," I said.

The consul smiled but registered my signed declaration and made out a passport in my married name.

"I must warn you," he said, "you might find yourself unable to cross the German-French border with your two passports. I cannot put a visa on your German passport that I do not recognize, you understand, and the Germans won't put a visa on your French passport that they do not recognize."

I did not tell him, but I was not worried. A few years back, in Fascist Rome, I had been able to convince a high official of my innocence when it had been discovered that I had overstayed my visa by six months. The bored employees I had seen at the French-German border could not be that difficult to deal with.

We left for Yugoslavia in June. At first the lushness and fertility of the countryside surprised us. We had expected the aridity of Greece and southern Italy.

We rushed like tourists through the ancient fortifications of Dubrovnik and the glorious fruit and flower market of Zagreb. We had little time. We swore we would come back.

The day we entered the bazaar of Sarajevo, Abel opened his sketchbook and I knew we would not go any farther. To us, this was the fabulous world of the Orient. Muslim merchants, taciturn and solemn in their colorful garb, sat among treasures: Persian rugs, carved chests, fabulous jewels, and embroidered things we could not identify. Over everything, the mysterious glow from gilded lamps and the scents of incense and Oriental coffee.

One day we stopped to buy cigarettes at a small store close to the bazaar entrance. The tiny place was crowded with plump bags resembling bags of rice. Lolling on top of them was the merchant in modern dark clothes, a fez askew on his head.

Soon Abel and the merchant were conversing in a mixture of German, French, English, and Greek. Abel said he wanted to travel to the Orient. The merchant sat up.

"I can arrange," he said. "You visit Afghanistan, Turkey, China. Ja, ja. I can arrange. You carry bundle. Sometimes you have camel, horse, donkey. Up mountains you have back. Ja, ja. You strong man."

A Merchant in the Bazaar of Sarajevo, *1939 (watercolor)*

The merchant clapped his hands. Almost instantly, a nimble girl of about twelve was at the door. Long, flowing black pantalets, embroidered crimson vest, white scarf knotted on top of her head that left her dark hair to fall free. The merchant lazily showed three fingers of his left hand. The girl ran, came back a few minutes later carrying three tiny cups of thick, fragrant coffee on a brass tray.

"And my wife?" Abel said.

"Oh, *facile*," the merchant said. "Wife go to spy school in Cairo. Four years. Good for woman, spy school!"

"What is in the bundle?" Abel asked. "Gold?"
"Better, better," the merchant said, smiling.

A not-very-distant day would arrive when to become an opium smuggler and a student spy in Cairo would seem better paths to follow than the road into darkness that suddenly opened.

X

❧

"I want to stay in Sarajevo," I told Abel the day before we returned to Germany.

"So do I," Abel said.

Six months, Abel had promised. We would not stay more than six months on German soil. Five months had already passed. I knew Abel had not forgotten. Neither he nor I ever mentioned the promise.

Back in my foreign home, I tried to respect the German vegetarian laws and taboos Christine had taught me as I cooked vegetables without killing them by overheating, baked bread without yeast and pies without much fat or sugar. I learned to do the laundry in the old time-consuming manner, and how to press the starched cuffs and collars of men's shirts.

One day around lunchtime, a young man came to demonstrate the use of a vacuum cleaner.

Abel came in.

"My mother never owned a vacuum cleaner," he said. "My wife does not need one."

And I knew that the man I had just married would probably not make a very good husband. I would not let the thought disturb me. It was better, I reasoned, not to burden ourselves with unnecessary possessions. Abel worked long hours at the agency, long hours every night at home doing freelance work. He never complained. I would not either.

Our lives had changed so completely and abruptly, it was as if we had, all of a sudden, reached old age. The only solace now was walking in the pleasant countryside on Sunday afternoons and remembering, remembering, a past so different from the present that it seemed as distant and irretrievable as a dream.

I took a few German lessons that were disappointing, slow, and boring. I decided to use my own empirical method. I listened stoically to conversations I did not understand and read, or rather deciphered, one book after another. Soon the written words began to make sense. And one day, at a family gathering, I spoke.

"You knew German before you came to this country," declared Abel's older sister.

In July we received an invitation to the French consulate for Bastille Day celebrations.

We danced to French music. We sang the *Marseillaise* heartily but not too well, and we drank champagne. I was eager to meet the French citizens of Stuttgart. They were few. I remember speaking to an attractive young woman.

"I have already five children," she said. "I never go out."

"I have made two hundred jars of marmalade and stored them in the cellar of the consulate," the consul's vivacious wife said.

One German, an invited official, brown shirt, boots, and ruddy face, sat alone, staring at the cup of champagne set in front of him on a small round table. Suddenly he reached for the cup, emptied it in one gulp, gagged, got redder, glared at everybody.

Two weeks later, we were invited to a reception for the wedding of the consul's daughter.

We danced and drank champagne. The very young bride, I remember, was playful, the groom, an Argentinean businessman, was serious, and the consul and his wife were strangely distracted.

It must have been about a week later, at the beginning of August, that I had lunch with a young secretary from the French consulate. I have forgotten her name and her face but not her parting words.

"I am glad we had this meal together. We might never see each other again, you know," she said.

As soon as Abel came home that evening, I asked him what he thought of the young secretary's pessimistic words.

"Oh, yes, yes, I know, I too heard some saber rattling," Abel said. "Don't worry, the ogre has to digest Austria and Czechoslovakia first, and that will take time."

XI

❧

I rarely ventured out alone into the foreign world that Germany still was for me. Abel, who was working sixteen hours a day in order to escape this very world, had no time—and no desire—to take me out.

We visited his kind old mother. When younger brother, cocky in his uniform, would show up, we would leave abruptly and feel bad about it.

The friend who had persuaded Abel to return to Germany was now passing on to him the freelance jobs he did not want. We had to be grateful. Not easy. I disliked the man's wife as much as I disliked him. Moreover, we now knew that he was a party member. Our rare visits were strained.

I looked forward to the spartan vegetarian dinners at Christine's house. Christine was friendly and protective. She smiled at my French weaknesses, my pretty, unpractical dresses and shoes. And my waist. My liver had no room, she said. She had often massaged me to correct the defect when I was her patient.

One August evening at Christine's dinner table, I related that I had seen, pinned up on the wall of my dentist's office, newspaper clippings representing gruesome photographs of old German men and women who had been tortured by the cruel Poles.

"I bet these are the same newspaper clippings that were shown before we felt obligated to invade Czechoslovakia," Christine exclaimed.

The maid, we all knew, was listening.

Christine did not care; she loudly predicted future calamities.

The next morning, newspapers and a blaring radio in the center of town announced that the Poles had attacked a German radio station across the German-Polish border. The following day, the first of September, at 4:30 A.M., German tanks rolled into Poland.

Two days later, Abel came home in midmorning.

"Call, call the French consul . . . now," he said with such urgency that I asked no questions.

We had no phone, but the lawyer who lived on the second floor had let us use his phone before. I rushed downstairs. The housekeeper, her eyes red from weeping, opened the door.

"My mother came from Poland," she said as she let me in.

The telephone rang long and shrill in the empty shell of the French consulate.

I dialed again and again. An icy clamp tightened around my heart. My country had declared war on my husband's country, as it had said it would if Germany attacked Poland.

XII

~✧~

emories of these long-past days are like singed photographs retrieved from the ruins of a house that has burned down. Oddly estranged, they still make me shudder.

Abel and I, sitting on a bench in a darkening park, tears running down our faces. Passersby look down at us. Very un-German indeed, to weep in public. I still remember what I was seeing through my tears: flames devouring all things dear to me, from Chartres's cathedral to my grandmother's house with its thatched roof.

I, dwarfed and alone, walking under a hundred giant streamers blood-red with black swastikas in a white circle—floating down Stuttgart's tall stone buildings in celebration of a bloody victory over the hapless Poles.

Abel and I, standing under golden autumn trees, plotting how to get hold of younger brother's gun. We needed a gun to end our own unbearable lives.

And then there was Abel's white-haired mother saying that things are never as bad as one imagines. She must have known. No, she did not, we said.

Christine, eyes flashing, asking, "What did I tell you?"

Her calm husband, shaking his head, telling us, "The French are too smart to want to die for Poland."

Maybe that was true. Days passed, and France and England, who had declared war, were not invading Germany as expected. One week passed, and Poland was crushed. One week! Russia lost no time in grabbing a large chunk of the vanquished country.

In the history book I had had in grade school, there was a picture I had not forgotten: Frederick the Great, king of Prussia, Catherine the Great, empress of Russia, and Maria-Theresa, archduchess of Austria, tearing apart a map of Poland.

This had happened in the eighteenth century. Was it Poland's fate to be torn apart by its neighbors?

We were all awed by the swiftness of the German victory. But of course, Poland was such a backward country. The Poles had attacked the mighty German tanks on horseback, with lances!

On October 6, in a long speech, Hitler made a formal proposal for peace. Most Germans, I think, believed he was sincere. Abel and I, bewildered as we were, hung on to every shred of hope. We knew that the information we were fed was truncated, biased, or false, yet what one hears often enough, one begins to believe.

"Lies, lies, lies," Christine said. "Some truths even are lies in disguise. French and English people don't want war, Hitler says. Do people of any country ever want to have their lives disrupted, their homes destroyed, their sons killed? The Germans don't want war either. Yet, we will get a big war. Hitler has tasted blood . . . he wants more of it."

We refused to be as pessimistic as Christine. Winter had come. Nothing had happened. Nothing would happen. The world was listening to reason.

XIII

❦

One morning in late November, the lawyer's housekeeper knocked on my door. She had good news for me, she said. She had been downtown shopping and had heard that one could now send letters to England and France.

"Take your letter to the post office," she added. "I think you'll need special stamps."

All communications with England and France had been cut after the declaration of war and, as far as I knew, were still cut. But I was only too ready to believe any good news. I had been worried about my parents and my friends. They, no doubt, imagined that I was incarcerated, perhaps mistreated.

I rushed home to write a reassuring letter. I was well and free to go wherever I wanted to, I wrote. Everybody was as nice and as helpful as before. I hoped that peace would prevail; nobody I knew in Germany wanted war against France, I wrote.

At the post office, the employee to whom I handed my letter said, besides an emphatic, "*Nein!*" something I could not understand. He did not understand my bad German either.

A large woman standing by offered help. Towering over me, she explained, in simple German, that I had been misinformed. No, no letter could be sent to France. She felt so sorry for me, she said. She assured me that no German man wanted to fight against any French man. She would like so much to help me, she said, but she did not know how.

We walked side by side for a while. Suddenly she said, "If I were you, I would go to the radio station and just ask permission to read my letter on the radio."

What a good idea! The helpful woman gave me directions, I thanked her, and I was on my way.

At the radio station, a doorkeeper directed me to a polite, well-groomed young gentleman in civilian clothes who spoke French and was eager to help. Would I leave my letter with him? he asked. Yes, I would. He promised I would hear from him shortly.

That evening, I told Abel about all I had accomplished by myself in just one half day.

If he had any misgivings, he did not say.

One day later, I was assigned, by telegram, a late-evening appointment at the radio station. I went alone, taking with me another letter I had written to my friends. At the radio station, the polite gentleman was beaming as he told me that I was welcome to read any letters I would like.

I stood alone in a large, dark room, in front of a microphone, and read my letters.

Because of the darkness and the silence, but mostly because of the late hour, I thought that this was direct broadcasting. I imagined my voice traveling through the vast darkness and reaching my father and my mother in the old house where I had lived the happiest days of my childhood with my beloved grandparents.

To make sure I would reach them, I would have to repeat the reading, I thought. But no, the polite gentleman said, this should do for the moment.

Of course, what I had done were recordings that would be played day and night, I soon discovered. We had no radio, but all the people we knew did. Sometimes, walking on the street, I would hear my voice.

One day I received an invitation for tea from a lady who wanted French lessons. I welcomed the diversion.

She was about my age, slim and elegant, and she spoke French quite well. We agreed to meet for tea once a week. I did not think she needed any lessons, I said.

We sat at a small table in her airy, pleasant apartment and had tea and excellent homemade pastries. She said she had heard me on the radio.

Suddenly she bent toward me, across the table. "You are being used, do you know that?" she whispered.

Christine was less polite. She appeared on our threshold one night, turned her back on me, and addressed Abel angrily. I could not understand her. I don't think Abel ever told me what Christine truly said.

Less than a week later, a letter came from one of Abel's brothers-in-law who lived in a town about three hundred kilometers away. He was coming to visit us, he wrote.

He was a career officer who, because of a heart defect, worked in an office for the army. I had met him once. I remembered an ugly man with a kind smile.

He arrived on the following Sunday in late afternoon. It was odd and a bit perturbing for me to see a German army officer taking off his verdigris military greatcoat in our home. He too felt awkward, he smiled a lot.

He sat at our small table for dinner, talked briefly about his wife, Abel's favored sister, and their son, a boy of nine. Then, bending over as if he were addressing the noodles and greens on his plate, he said, or rather grumbled, "Don't do a thing for those . . . people. You don't know them. We, in the army, we know them. Don't ever get into any kind of deal with them. Abel, do you understand?"

Yes, Abel said, he understood.

I said nothing, but I had understood.

A few days later, a telegram came assigning me a late-evening appointment at the radio station. Abel accompanied me.

The polite gentleman at the radio station, that evening, wore the black SS uniform that made Abel cringe. Smiling confidently, he handed me a prepared text, an appeal to French women, he announced.

"Oh no, no, I cannot read a text I have not written," I exclaimed.

The polite gentleman looked surprised and rather annoyed.

"Well, in the future, you will have to deal with someone else anyway," he finally said. "I am proud to inform you that I'll depart for the front shortly."

"The front, which front?" I asked.

I got no answer.

Another telegram summoned me sometime later. I went with Abel, who had to explain that I had a bad episode of a recurring laryngitis. I, of course, could not say a word.

Next I received a check. No explanation, just a check for what seemed, at the time, a substantial amount.

I returned the check, in person, to a very surprised employee.

A week or so later another check came. Again, I returned it.

No more telegrams or checks arrived after that.

"You take one step on your own and it is right onto treacherous sands," Christine told me. "Ask me for advice before you take another."

XIV

❧

I liked the cold, dry, sunny winter days in Stuttgart and the snow that softened the ponderous architecture of the town. The suburban houses too were more friendly when icicles dribbled in front of the scrubbed windows and the white fluff messed up the bushes in the front yards.

After my first misdirected efforts, I refused myself even the modest pleasure that a stroll could offer. I ventured out without Abel only for short errands to the grocery store or the vegetable market. And there, invariably having to make a choice between kohlrabi, cabbage, and rutabaga, I would get sick with longing for the cornucopia of a Parisian street market.

I did not go to Dr. Müller any longer. He was treating tuberculosis and kidney stones with herb tea and bicarbonate of soda, I had heard. I had lost faith in his doctoring.

Christine still believed in him. She also believed that if the Germans attacked France, they would be taught a lesson worse than the one they had been taught in 1918.

I did not.

I lived through the first month of 1940 hoping, dreaming that the war would never start, or trembling with fear that it would. If it did, I knew in my heart that France would be crushed. I could not explain how I knew, but I knew.

Christine said I was a defeatist.

On April 8, Germany invaded Norway.

"An ancient rite," Christine said. "Our noble ancestors always went on a rampage in the spring! That one will end up badly, I am afraid."

A few scattered bombs fell around the city. No mention was made in the newspaper.

Nobody seemed to worry. Strange. As if Norway had been a far-away country.

Abel read an ad in the newspaper: a grand piano was for sale in our neighborhood. We easily found the tall Gothic house with its high stained-glass windows. We rang the bell hanging by a heavy carved door of dark wood. A pale, unsmiling young woman opened it for us, and we saw the piano. It stood in a vast, bare room under the magic blue, red, and purple light from a stained-glass window. The high, vaulted ceiling above was lost in the shadows.

Abel sat at the piano and played. Mozart, Schumann, Beethoven.

Abel's mother and sisters had often told me how beautifully he could play. I had known him as a painter and had never heard him play anything besides dance music on an upright piano. Indeed, he could make great music.

Abel stopped playing. We exchanged only one look. He bought the piano.

The piano filled half of the largest room in our apartment. We had a small bench made to order. Once more, I wondered about the man I had married. He had refused to buy one chair, and now he was acquiring the most cumbersome piece of furniture.

Less than two weeks later, bombs fell on our area, and there was a crater-like hole in place of the only tall Gothic house in the vicinity.

X V

❦

On May 10, Germany invaded neutral, small, helpless Holland, Belgium, and Luxembourg.

Sonder Meldungs (special reports), preceded by a phrase of glorious music, followed one another, every one tightening the clamp around our hearts. We all knew that France's turn was next.

Abel could only share my anguish.

Christine, bitterly triumphant, had begun to pack up.

"They want it, they will get it," she said. "This city will be destroyed."

One month later, on June 14, the German army was clattering down the Champs Élysées.

No one had anticipated such a swift victory over France, the victorious least of all.

Younger brother was deeply disappointed in French men. "I had thought they were better fighters," he told me reproachfully. Over the years, many German men, upon learning I was French, imparted the same complaint to me.

Christine was surprised, she said, but she went on packing.

As for me, the defeatist, I had agonized for eight months over the war that we had seen coming and the defeat that would follow. Germany's astonishingly fast triumph came as a relief. For the moment at least. My worst nightmares had been swept away: neither Paris nor Chartres's cathedral nor my grandmother's thatched roof had gone up in flames. I was numbed, and, deep down, thankful.

For a while, I did not know that the *Blitzkrieg* had sent hordes of terrified refugees and retreating soldiers down the southward roads right through the area where my whole family lived. By the time I learned about it, newspapers were already picturing German soldiers as good Samaritans distributing food to French refugees and filling up their car tanks with gasoline so that they could drive back home.

Most Germans I met at the time hid from me their satisfaction at the triumph of their country over mine. A few offered sympathy. Christine's brother-in-law, a poet whom I had met twice and who was then a soldier, wrote to me that he had wept when his country's army had paraded down the Champs Élysées. I kept this letter, would burn it only when expecting the Gestapo to search my house, three years later.

Every day, through the fearful weeks, the lawyer's housekeeper put a cup of excellent coffee—coffee was already rationed—and pastries in front of my door, rang my doorbell, and ran before I could talk to her.

In July, there were rumors that the invasion of England was now imminent.

Weeks passed.

Then it was announced that since England stubbornly, foolishly refused to accept the peace that Germany had generously and repeatedly offered, Goering with his formidable Luftwaffe would teach her a lesson.

Sonder Meldungs resumed. Puny British airplanes fell from the sky by the hundreds, and, we were told, practically none of the powerful German ones went down.

After the total destruction of Coventry, a new German word was coined: *Coventryzieren.*

On August 25, British planes bombarded Berlin for the first time. Minimized, the event could not be denied.

Well-informed people had explained again and again that no enemy airplane could fly undetected over the ironclad German borders. Suddenly—a revelation—not only could enemy airplanes fly over German borders, they could fly unhindered over hundreds of kilometers of German territory! And not only one plane, many planes, big, heavy planes, bombers.

Germany was vulnerable after all.

"What did I tell you?" Christine asked. She went on packing. She alone was moving to the country house. Her husband would stay in town with some friends.

She offered to take me along.

"No, I could not leave Abel alone," I said.

"You'll join me someday," she predicted.

One beautiful morning, in early September, I think—the leaves on the trees were still green—I happened to be downtown when some units of the victorious army returning from France paraded down Main Street.

Tanks, guns, boots, songs—one sinister entity: the death machine that had trampled down my country.

The solace of tears was not for me that day. My heart had hardened. *Their hour shall come,* something in me said.

Strange, that at such a moment I should find hope. Or was Christine's bitter faith contagious?

XVI

The piano had transformed our lives.

Abel played the music I loved—classical. Waves of harmonies flowed from under his strong artist's hands with an ease I could not comprehend. He played as if this were the easiest, the most natural thing in the world to do. And once more he seemed to be the carefree, happy man I had met five years before under more merciful skies.

Our hopes of getting out of Germany shelved for the time being, he played the piano from the moment he came home until late in the evening, taking only a short time for supper. The lawyer who lived on the second floor right under us only said, and with a smile, that he preferred Mozart to scales. But as it would always be with us—the moment of happiness was short.

One day, in a state of rare agitation, Abel came home shortly before noon. He could not have waited until evening, he said, to tell me what had happened.

Early that morning, he had been summoned to the offices of the Gestapo. There, a handsome gentleman with icy blue eyes dressed in smart civilian gray, "a real aristocrat," had received him and offered armchair, cognac, cigarettes. Then, leisurely, he had indicated that he knew everything about Abel and his wife: education, diverse occupations and talents, travels, long stay in France, sojourn in a Spanish jail. . . .

"The Fatherland needs men like you," he had suddenly declared.

After a lengthy pause, the man had explained: "You will go back to France as a painter. Don't visit your wife's family. With your engineering background, you will be able to gather information that is of interest to us. You will be rewarded handsomely. And, as you know, Germany's might shall be behind you at all times."

Abel had understood the offer only too well. How was he to get out of this situation intelligently?

"Can you keep a secret from your wife?" the Gestapo agent asked.

"No, I can't," Abel said. Too fast, perhaps. "And then, and then, I talk in my sleep. . . . When I was a child . . ."

"Enough," the Gestapo agent interrupted, and he took away cognac and cigarettes. "For the time being . . . we will let you go. I warn you, this interview is top secret."

What he really said was: *"Wir werden sie an die Wand stehen lassen"* (We will let you lean against the wall)—which ominously resembles: *"Wir werden sie an die Wand stellen,"* meaning: "We will shoot you."

"Who do they think they are?" Abel asked angrily.

But I knew he was frightened. So was I. "They" knew all about us! We looked at our own walls with a new distrust, felt shadowed walking on the streets side by side, hardly dared to talk freely even when surrounded by trees alone.

As time passed and nothing else happened, we became carefree again—as animals do, I suppose, when scents left by the hunter have blown away.

The war had gone south for the winter. Germans, British, Italians were fighting in Greece, Albania, and North Africa—Ethiopia, Libya, Algeria, Morocco.

In the Atlantic Ocean, a sneaky war went on. German U-boats sank many vessels, mostly British. *Sonder Meldungs*, several times a day, gloated over numberless sinkings.

At his office, Abel announced that, according to his calculations, there would very soon be practically no enemy boats left to sink.

"What a shame," he said. "Our brave U-boats are going to be completely idle."

Christine's husband urged me to persuade Abel not to make sarcastic remarks at the office. He would hate, he said, to lose a good worker.

Christine had moved to her house in the hilly country away from any large city. We saw her husband more often now. Because he was a businessman, he had to be a member of the Nazi Party, but he did not approve of the party's brutal ways. Of course, he hoped Germany would win the war. Abel and I hoped Germany would lose the war. I avoided controversial subjects of conversation. Abel did not.

In April, Hitler had to help Mussolini, who was losing battle after battle in Greece. He invaded Greece and Yugoslavia and within two weeks had occupied both.

Sonder Meldungs. Sonder Meldungs.

On June 22, Hitler attacked the Soviet Union on a 3,500-kilometer front, from the Baltic Sea to the Black Sea.

The advance of the German armies at first was tremendous. By mid-October they had come within a hundred kilometers of Moscow.

"Christmas in Moscow," was the battle cry.

Only 129 years had passed since Napoléon's mighty army had reached Moscow, found a country devastated by its own people, a city burned to the ground, and retreated. The Russian winter had put a bitter end to Napoléon's astounding conquests.

The Germans had not forgotten Napoléon. "But," they explained to me, "Hitler was another kind of conqueror, a modern conqueror who possessed modern means. And anyway, what had been disastrous for Napoléon's army was the retreat. The Germans do not retreat."

It must have been about this time that the first German movie in color was shown in Stuttgart. A movie in color—we had to see it, even though the title made us wary: *Jude Süss*. No fiction this, but the true story of a Jew who had, around the turn of the century, I think, become prime minister to the good, naive king of Württemberg. This Jew, of course, had been a dissolute, despicable individual. And a thief. And a cad. He had wasted the citizens' money. He had raped a beautiful, innocent Christian girl. . . . Finally he had been hanged. I remember the bare feet of the hanged man dangling in the air. This last image enlarged. Very effective: the audience burst into applause, and I got sick to my stomach. Abel quickly led me out. The attendants, with the reverence accorded only to pregnant women, opened the doors for us. The energetic clapping was still going on as we reached the street.

XVII

One afternoon in late summer, I got into a long conversation with a young woman who lived close by. I don't know how we got to talk. I had seen her often, but in Germany at the time one did not speak to a person to whom one had not been introduced.

"I am young, I have no children, I'll be required to work in an ammunition factory for sure," the young woman confided at some point. "But if you study something you are protected," she added. "And so I am learning hand-weaving at the trade school."

"I am young, I have no children. . . . I think hand-weaving is something I ought to learn," I told Abel that evening.

He agreed.

The next day, I registered at the Kunstgewerbeschule, which was within walking distance, a tall, square building with many large windows. The classrooms had very high ceilings so that the school was higher than a four-story building would usually be.

Hand-weaving was taught in a large room on the top floor. There were three upright looms for tapestry-making, a half-dozen flat looms for fabric-weaving, and long tables at which students painted tiny white and red squares on lined paper—weaving patterns. For the first weeks, I was put to painting countless weaving patterns. Tedious. But I was promised it would not last.

There were few students in the hand-weaving section and only one teacher, a short middle-aged woman who wore the party badge.

It must have been in November that the principal owner of the advertising agency where Abel worked invited us to a party he was giving at his house in honor of a special visitor from Berlin.

Abel declared that we were not going.

I was tired of never going to anything, I wanted to go.

I still wish we had not.

The house of the agency's owner was located in the northern hilly suburbs, as was our apartment, but in the wealthy section, quite a distance away. We enjoyed the quiet walk along a road that meandered between gardens. The night was clear and cold over the darkened city below in the valley.

The moment we entered the spacious living room, Abel got tense. A man was barking into a telephone. The women in one area, the men in another were silent. Our host whispered that the man on the phone, his guest of honor, was one of Hitler's first sixty companions.

"*Sehr schön!*" Abel sneered.

We were offered cognac and champagne. Both French. I asked for water. I never touched any of the looted food or drink from France.

"He was talking to Berlin," a woman, duly awed, whispered as the guest of honor finally hung up. He was of medium build, stooped slightly, had no distinctive features except his grating voice. A burly, tall man stood or sat by his side at all times.

Bottles and glasses were put in front of them by the host himself, their glasses filled with champagne. They toasted each other, I didn't understand why, and the other guests raised their glasses, but not Abel and I.

Conversations grew louder—I did not try to follow except when somebody brought up the "Jewish problem."

At every gathering I had attended, somebody invariably had brought up the "Jewish problem."

"I know the solution," the guest of honor announced loudly.

Expectant silence fell.

"A crematory! Give me a good crematory . . . and, one after another . . ."

Uneasy silence followed.

I saw Abel striding across the room. He reached the corner table and bent toward the guest of honor.

"*Du, ich möchte dich was sagen. Du bist ein idiot, und dein Adolf auch!*" ("You, I want to tell you something. You are an idiot, and your Adolf also!" The use of the familiar *du* instead of the formal *Sie* was intentionally insulting.) And he slapped the man's face.

The burly man had stood up. Abel fell across the table. There was a sound of breaking glass.

All the men in the room rushed toward the corner table.

"Drunk, he is drunk. Drunk . . . drunk," several voices said.

I stood alone in the middle of the room staring at a wall of men's backs. The group of women had shrunk to nothing in a corner.

"Drunk . . . drunk . . . is drunk."

Suddenly someone was pushing me through a small door out into the icy night. Then Abel was pushed out, our coats and hats thrown after us. Fruit trees rigid with cold stood all around us.

"Run!" I think it was the voice of Christine's husband that said, "Run!"

I don't know whether we did. But we were out of the orchard when we heard the back door reopen.

"Sie werden vernichted sein" ("You will be destroyed"), a grating voice in the night promised us several times.

Many years later, I would sometimes hear that voice at night. I don't anymore.

Abel had not calmed down. He was twisting his good hat, trying to tear it apart.

"Don't say anything, don't," he said, perhaps expecting the little housewife to reproach him.

"I did not slap him hard enough."

"Somebody tripped you. . . ."

"I did not slap him hard enough. . . ."

He threw his hat over a fence.

"The poor Jews, the poor Jews," he said with renewed anger in his voice.

"Do you think they would . . . ?"

"No, of course not. They would not dare. But I cannot permit anybody to make such a boast in my presence. That's all."

A while later, he said, "Please don't say anything, don't."

After that, what we had begun to call animal fear sat by our side. For a long time. We never spoke of it.

Later, Christine's husband reported some gossip: the "guest of honor" was, had been for some time, in trouble—the rivalries among the men at the top were fierce. He might have neither time nor power for revenge.

I think it was around that time that Abel began to mention his guardian angel.

XVIII

We went on with our lives, as most of us do. Anger, terror, and doubts disguised, buried under the vulgar necessities that daily survival demands.

Some, the brave perhaps, chose to die.

A few days after the dismal party, the lady with whom I sometimes had tea and conversations in French related, with more pride than sorrow, that two of her school friends, young army officers, had committed suicide.

Not so long before, Abel and I had been about to do the same. But we had not. Why? Hope. Hope, stronger than reason.

At the advertising agency, Abel went on working, harder than before. Younger artists had been enlisted, and the newly hired young women had little experience. In the evening, he played the piano, at times with savage energy.

My weaving at the school was more difficult than I had imagined. On the flat loom, I had started to weave a simple rug with rough brown yarn made of cow hair. The loom was less than one meter wide, yet my shuttle kept jumping out and landing on the floor, and the chain's threads broke too often.

On the half-meter-wide upright loom, I was to weave a tapestry. I had, with Abel's help, drawn on cardboard the sketch ("cartoon" in the trade) that would be placed behind the chain as a guide.

The other students favored geometric or decorative motives. I had decided on colorful fish enjoying their brief, free lives in deep waters.

The material I had to work with was a big bundle of short pieces of fine wool of all shades and colors. Quite beautiful.

The procedure, deceptively simple, the teacher said, was the famous French Gobelin procedure. It consisted of slipping a single yarn of colored wool between every thread of the chain (real hand-weaving). Then patting down every yarn against the preceding one with a metal tool shaped somewhat like a table fork. If the patting was not done correctly, the tapestry would wobble.

It was slow, yes. But curiously satisfying.

After a few days, I already had a few centimeters of water alive with such interesting shadings of blues and greens. Soon I would start on the happy fish.

December 7, my birthday. I had already lost all interest in birthday festivities. So had Abel.

Two days later, we knew that on the other side of the world, a man-made disaster had taken place that triggered rejoicing in the part of the world we reluctantly belonged to. Pearl Harbor. A poetic name for a catastrophic dawn mirrored in the tropical waters of the Pacific Ocean.

Japan, on the map a mere cluster of small islands, had gone to war against China and the United States of America, two countries as vast as continents. These were events that belonged to a quasi-fabulous faraway world. But then the improbable rushed closer: Hitler and Mussolini declared war on the United States of America!

Only ten years had passed since I had closed a thousand-page book—*History and Geography of the U.S.A.*—that I had had to read in the girls' college of Chartres. In high school, I had drawn, not once but many times, the map of the U.S.A. and all its rivers, mountains, cities, products, industries. . . . I knew about the natural resources of the vast country.

Did Hitler know as much?

Most Germans showed pride when their *Führer* declared war on the U.S.A.

I remember walking on the streets of Stuttgart on a cold December day, wanting to read faces.

Housewives were scurrying for food to put on the table. Shortages were severe already. No time for thinking. The *Führer* knows best.

A young soldier stood at the back of a trolley, smiling. As I climbed in, I read the inscription on his belt buckle: *"Gott mit uns"* ("God with us").

Which God? Wotan? I too smiled.

Sedate old gentlemen took their daily walk—loden coats, canes, felt hats of a subdued green. Their shaded faces told nothing.

But some of them, perhaps many, thought what I thought: "Today, the end begins."

Only twenty-four years before, my father, as secretary of City Hall in a small French village, had hoisted the U.S. flag way up on City Hall's high roof. Later on, my young socialist father, the old reactionary mayor, and my conservative grandfather had stood together in the yard and, looking up, had for one blessed moment—and I with them—smiled the same smile.

I was eight, I remembered.

That December day in 1941, on a cold German street, I knew the same dizzy, blind confidence in the happy ending.

How good that I did not know how long and treacherous the way would be.

XIX

❦

I was now working on my tapestry every day. Fish, three so far, were taking shape. A bit rigid, perhaps, for frolicking fish, but their exuberant colors, reds, oranges, yellows, told how happy they were.

All the students worked at different looms, on different projects, and at a distance from each other. All were polite and quiet. I was the only foreigner.

The young woman who had told me about the art trade school was also working on a tapestry—disquieting squares of stark white, purple, and yellow. I could not bring myself to ask her what it wanted to say.

Another young woman was weaving, on the flat loom, a blanket for the baby she was expecting. She used her own yarns to weave bold stripes of blue, green, purple with a silver thread here and there. The baby blanket would not be very practical, but it would be beautiful.

I expressed my admiration.

"That's what the Indians of Peru did to me," the future mother said, laughing. "I was born in Peru, lived there until the age of fifteen."

A tall blond about my age was finishing a large tapestry for her master's degree. A good, solid, unadventurous, ornamental motif, dark red on off-white. A technically perfect work: edges straight and even, no wobbling anywhere.

I praised the piece once as I passed by. The girl became very friendly, invited me for dinner at her mother's house. I cannot remember how I managed not to go. The girl wore the party badge.

I always arrived early at the school. One morning in mid-December, there was only one student in the classroom when I came in—the tall blond. She was not at her loom but stood in front of one of the large windows at the far end of the room, intently looking down.

There had not been much to look at on the grounds, where a garden show had taken place two years earlier in the summer of 1939. Bare flower beds, raked regularly, meandering paths swept clean, low buildings erected for the show, now empty, clean and cold.

I walked to the window closest to my loom.

On that December morning, 1941, the doors of some buildings were wide open. People, each carrying a small suitcase, were walking out and climbing into buses parked at some distance.

The proceedings were quiet and orderly—as they usually were in Germany.

From the top floor of the tall school building, in the December morning light, I could not see people's faces well, or the details of their clothing.

A short man in a too-large hat stopped in his tracks halfway to the bus, then resumed his walk. Did he wear an armband with the yellow star? I was not sure. Suddenly I had to know where these people were going. I turned toward the tall blond girl. She was about ten meters away from where I stood, her head leaning against the windowpane. She was weeping. I saw the tears on her cheeks.

She must have felt my eyes on her. She turned away and ran out of the room. The classroom door slammed behind her.

I followed, but not fast enough: the hall was empty. There were doors left and right. I opened the door closest to me and bumped into the teacher coming out.

"What are you doing here?" she asked. "Go to your work."

"Where are they going? The people . . ."

"Which people?"

"The people down there . . . Did they spend the night in those cold buildings?" I was incoherent, I knew, but I also sensed that the teacher knew what I was talking about.

"What? What did you say? Those buildings can be heated."

"But the people," I insisted, "the people who were climbing into buses . . ."

"Oh, those people. Calm down. They are being relocated. Don't worry, everything is all right." The teacher smiled and patted me on the back. "Go back to your work."

Students were arriving. None had seen anybody climbing into buses. The buses had all departed by now. The gates to the former garden show were closed, the buildings' doors shut.

The blond girl did not show up for a few days. Her finished tapestry was taken down after class. By the time I saw her again, I had calmed down. The people I had seen had not looked upset. They had walked out of the buildings I had no reason to decide were unheated. Overnight bags in hand, they had climbed into buses. What was wrong with that? They had acted like people who knew where they were going. Why had I been so upset? My behavior had been ridiculous. The blond girl had wept. Well, maybe a friend of hers had been among the people who had departed. She had run away from me in shame because she had realized I had seen her weeping. The Germans were that way.

. . .

All this reasoning was done as I was working on my tapestry, finishing a fourth happy fish, weaving a few centimeters of water. When the water turned a murky gray-green, I started on a fish that took up almost the width of the tapestry. The big fish in dull yellows and sick greens swelled up. Went belly-up.

"What's that?" the usually cool and collected teacher exclaimed. "You did not follow your drawing. Why? Why?"

"Don't know."

"Stop it. Right now. Your tapestry is finished."

A strange piece of work, indeed. I did not know what to think of it myself. Would not for several years.

Classes recessed for the Christmas vacation.

X X

ecember 20, 1941. The German soldiers on the Russian front knew by now that they would not feast on Christmas in Moscow as promised but instead would be left to the mercies of "General Winter."

The major setback in Russia, added to the insane declaration of war on the U.S.A., could have been ample cause for Abel and me to rejoice. That is, if we had not known many of the poor devils, forbidden to retreat, now condemned to freeze and die in their summer uniforms.

To mask the importance of the failure to take Moscow as planned, the propaganda machine vaunted the successful offensive in the Ukraine. The Soviets, knowing they would never return, we were told, had blown up their own enormous, vital dam on the Dnieper. The victorious German army, having conquered the Ukraine, was on its way to the Caucasus. Germany now possessed the wheat of the Ukraine and the oil of the Caucasus. Well . . . almost.

And then there was the stunning advance in Africa. And the victories of Germany's brave Japanese allies—rebaptized "Honorary Aryans"—all over Asia.

Herzliche Weihnachten! (Merry Christmas!)

The sacrifices the Motherland demanded were to be borne proudly and silently.

Christine wrote from a ski resort in Tirol, Austria, inviting us to join her for the holiday. Her husband disliked skiing and did not want to go, but Abel and I were soon on our way.

The ski resort was pleasantly rustic, the hotel comfortable, and Christine was in an unusually relaxed mood. Skiing promised to be poor; a warm wind had started to blow and the snow was melting in patches.

On the second day, Abel got irritated when he caught sight of Christine conversing amiably with a heavyset individual in a brown uniform with a strange yellowish face that, I fancied, had been punched at birth.

"A brute's face," Abel said, and he warned Christine that he did not want to be introduced.

Christine laughed.

"I enjoy studying a grown-up man with the mental age of a child," she said.

"And I am doing my best to stay away, precisely, from such a species," Abel said. "We are leaving."

The next morning, we were on the train for Sankt Anton, another resort Abel knew. There we rented a room from a widow who ran her tiny farmhouse at the edge of the valley, kilometers away from village and big hotel. Not one uniform there to mar the gorgeous snow.

We had four exhilarating days.

We returned to Stuttgart only to find the *Stellungs Befehl* for Abel in our mailbox. He should have presented himself for military duty five days before.

Abel laughed.

I did not.

"Don't you see, they did not catch me!" he said. "Anyway, this is a mistake. First, I am nearly forty, and then, all men my age have had military training. I have not, since I was out of the country. It's a mistake."

The next morning, he handed the orders to the advertising agency's principal owner, who did not share Abel's cheerful mood at all. He at once left for the *Kommandantur*, the *Stellungs Befehl* in his briefcase.

The following day, he reported drily: "Fixed for now. Don't ask me to do it again."

Once, in an unguarded moment, Christine's husband told Abel: "You have cost us a bunch, you know."

We never tried to learn how much money that was.

At the end of February, *Sonder Meldungs* announced the victories of the invincible warriors, our Japanese friends. They had landed on Java and, in the process, annihilated an entire enemy fleet of cruisers and destroyers, American, British, Dutch, Australian. . . .

A propitious time, the owners of the advertising agency decided, and they made an appointment for me with the high-ranking officer in charge of the recruiting office of the army. I was to explain to him how essential my husband was for the survival of their business!

I must have been briefed about the importance this agency had for the defense of the Fatherland, but I don't remember any of it. I remember being highly amused by the bizarre scheme—and curious.

The German officer turned out to be a short, older man in a much-decorated verdigris uniform, sitting at a well-shined desk that seemed a bit too high for him.

He had gotten all his decorations in the First World War, fighting my country, I thought. He probably thought of that too. He listened to my French-accented German, nodded, smiled a little, stiffly grandfatherly, polite.

I can't remember one single word we said. Nobody ever knew, I suppose, how persuasive I had been.

For the whole month of January, back at school, I was put to painting weaving patterns: hundreds of tiny red squares alternating with white ones and arranged into neat geometric patterns.

Nobody told me this was a punishment, but it surely felt like one.

In February, I learned to spin with artificial yarn. Harder to do than to spin with wool, even the teacher said so. But there was no wool. Anyway, I was not very good.

One afternoon, students and teachers were summoned down to the large auditorium to hear speeches.

I no longer remember what was said, but I remember what I saw: a middle-aged professor stood in front of a lectern and spoke in a measured tone when suddenly a booted young thug in a brown uniform stepped to the podium, pushed the professor aside, took his place, and shouted and jerked his arms for half an hour.

The professor stood by meekly, his head bent.

Most shocking was the passivity of the audience. Were these accepted proceedings? Was I the only one horrified? No one I talked to seemed to share my feelings, or dared to express an opinion.

I refrained from telling Abel about the incident. He was angry enough already.

It must have been in March that I was finally permitted to weave on the horizontal loom again.

"One cushion," the teacher said. "One cushion" meant no more than sixty centimeters. There was a shortage of yarn.

I "made yarn" at home by unraveling some sweaters. Since I was short and slim I could weave enough for "three cushions" or one skimpy dress for myself.

There was no longer any fabric for sale in the stores.

My skill had improved. I could weave faster now. One day I discovered, at the bottom of a closet, some bright red artificial yarn that had been discarded, I guessed, because of its offensive color. Something had gone wrong with the dye, I was told.

I liked the bright red and wove enough for two big cushions before anybody noticed. I added a bright blue stripe, then a white stripe, then a red one. Blue, white, red.

A student with whom I had so far mostly exchanged only polite greetings stopped by my loom.

"The colors of the French flag," she said. "And what are you going to make with that?"

"A nice wide skirt," I said. "That way, there will be one French flag on the streets of Stuttgart."

The student walked away.

The next morning, the teacher came up to me as I was taking off my coat.

"It has just been discovered that your age is above the regular age for admission to our school," she said slowly, clearly, as if afraid I would not understand. "Finish that piece." She pointed at the blue, white, red on the loom, "And pack up your things."

It would have been useless to protest.

I packed up: a small tapestry with a cryptic message, brushes, red ink, a whole copybook of useless weaving patterns, and a fancy French flag.

Weaving at the big loom, Sankt Peter, 1942

An older student stopped by. We had often exchanged smiles but never spoken. She dressed a little like a farm girl.

She handed me a slip of paper.

"It's the address of a weaving shop," she explained, "up north near the border with Denmark, on a farm. Write to the owner, tell her you are French, she will hire you."

This was a bit odd and unexpected, and I smiled as I said thanks.

"I don't think that I am good enough," I said.

"Tell her you are French," the girl whispered as she walked away.

XXII

❧

Christine's husband asked me, "for the last time," he said, to persuade Abel to be more careful in front of people at work. An employee there, apparently, had reported about a "savage" air raid on Berlin by British barbarians.

"Did they cross our borders again?" Abel had asked with feigned amazement. "Ah, these British barbarians, they would *Coventryzieren* Berlin, they would! Oh! But we won't let them."

I laughed.

"This is no laughing matter," the harassed businessman said wearily. "Ah, yes, I know about your French flag . . . and my wife, my wife. . . ." He held his head in both hands.

Christine, pretending she wanted to save money, had decided to make the large Nazi flag that had to be displayed over the rooftop of their country house. Christine, who could draw, paint, and sew beautifully, fabricated a Nazi flag with a swastika that looked like a vicious spider. The flag had waved for three days over the rooftop. Some villagers had complained, and now the police were investigating.

"When will you people understand that you are not helping anybody with jokes and pranks? When?" Christine's husband asked.

. . .

Aformer employee of the advertising agency whom Abel had liked and who had, for unknown reasons, dropped out of sight for several months, rang our bell late one evening. I had only heard about him, never met him. He was slightly older than Abel, shared his convictions, and had been, I knew, very outspoken about them.

As soon as he was behind closed doors, he whispered, "I was in a concentration camp—or better said, hell—for three months."

"Ah, nobody knew where you were," Abel also whispered.

"And you still don't know ... understand? Could happen to you too. Or worse ... But listen, there is a haven. That's what I came to tell you." Resuming a normal tone of voice, our visitor went on, "You remember Dr. Todt, the famous engineer who built our superhighways? His offices are now a branch of government, the Organization Todt, OT for short. The OT rebuilds roads, bridges, railroad tracks destroyed during the fighting, builds fortifications—some thousand bunkers on the Atlantic coast in France—cuts forests in the occupied countries. In Finland, for example, where I was not long ago taking pictures. Yes, I have become a photographer for the OT!" He pulled some large photographs out of his briefcase.

"Look at these: a wood convoy in Finland." And whispering again, "I suggest that you make drawings from these photographs. Do a fine portrait of that man here, and of that one there. They are influential OT men roughing it. Understand? Nice portraits, a bit flattering ... not too much. Send your drawings to this man at the headquarters in Berlin." He indicated a name written on the back of one photograph. "*Viel Glück!*"

Our visitor got up. He had been sitting on the piano bench. He laid two photographs on the piano, said good-bye, and walked down our narrow hall toward the door.

"*Viel Glück*," he said again as he walked out.

"Who is he really?" I wondered.

Abel still stood in front of the closed door as if unwilling to move. "Guardian angel," he whispered.

Abel did exactly what had been suggested.

We waited. Not for long. Summoned by telegram to OT's Berlin headquarters, Abel was back after only a few days. He had been hired for four months as a *Künstlerischer Bildberichterstatter* (artistic pictorial reporter).

He would be sent on assignments. Every picture he would bring back would be the property of the OT. He would be paid a salary equal to the salary he had been receiving from his former employers.

We had been hoping, wishing for a change. Suddenly there it was, leaving us amazed, elated, and anxious.

I was not going to be left alone in Stuttgart. I at once wrote to Frau Benzler, the weaving-shop owner, applying for a job as a weaver. I was not highly skilled, I wrote, and I was French.

Frau Benzler answered by return mail. Yes, indeed, she needed one more weaver for the summer months. She was retaining a room for me at the house of "Fisherman Schulz," a neighbor.

We said a few good-byes.

Abel's mother was dignified and kind as usual. I knew how proud and fond of Abel she was, the best of all her children, she had once told me. Looking at her, I wished again I that would someday possess her beautiful white hair and also some of her calm strength.

She was a bit confused by my departure.

"Shouldn't a soldier's wife stay home and wait for her man?" she wondered.

"I am not a soldier, Mother! I have been hired as an artistic reporter for four months by the OT, not by the army."

Younger brother had been enlisted but was still in training. He had recently come home on furlough. "He looked so handsome!" his young wife said. "And he was so proud of his soldier's uniform."

On April 23, 1942, we took a train from Stuttgart's stately railroad station.

"I think the architect dreamed he was building a Gothic church when he made the plans for this railroad station," I said.

"Pretentious, ugly," Abel said.

"No, it's not ugly."

"German megalomania!"

Arguing was better than talking about the near future.

I don't remember much of the trip. I was used to traveling by train. There was not much difference between French and German railroad stations or trains. Except that in Germany everything, from platforms to train compartments and toilets, looked heavier, cleaner, and more secure. Also less inviting.

There were few travelers that day. None seemed to be in a hurry, uncertain of a goal, or lost. There were some uniforms, officers mostly.

We sat together as far as Sweinfurt, I think, where we separated. There my memory has kept one image: Abel's handsome, pensive profile behind a window as his train pulled away, bound for Berlin. But even that image is blurred. I probably fought too hard to keep tears from running down my face.

I am sure I took a train bound for Hamburg, and a trolley to Abel's old friend's house somewhere in the suburbs.

The old friend, Hans W., had freed Abel from the Gestapo in 1936 after the dismal adventure in Spain. A kind, pensive older man who grew rare plants and collected insects. I was meeting him and his wife for the first time, but they both welcomed me as a friend. I spent several days in their neat, suburban house and lovely garden.

They strolled with me through the streets, and I saw for the first time the effects of an air raid. Four-story townhouses had been reduced to piles of rubble, or to odd ruins that looked like giant decayed teeth. Some were hollowed out, only their blind facades still standing. The harbor and boats I wanted to see were far beyond walls of cranes, repair equipment, and barriers. We could hear hammering and pounding as we walked by a park where several plaster or concrete giant dinosaurs stood undisturbed.

"There are no workers repairing the damaged houses," I said. "Why?"

"A harbor is essential, houses are not," Hans said. "And anyway, this air raid was only a prelude."

One evening, Hans and his wife took me for dinner to the house of their best friends, a pleasant couple in their sixties. I remember their dining room as if I had been there yesterday. Oversized, with an oblong table, tall, heavy chairs, high, stark white walls decorated exclusively with crossed rapiers, twelve of them, long and pointed. Antiques, black with age.

A fitting decor for the table talk entirely about the war, the murderers at the helm, and the catastrophic future. The men grew angrier as they spoke. The wives tried in vain to make them lower their voices.

"Why did you come to our godforsaken country!" they asked.

None of my explanations would satisfy them.

XXIII

❧

The train trip from Hamburg to Sankt Peter, a small town on the North Sea coast, I have forgotten. But not the area I reached, a flat land of a subdued green sparsely dotted with low white farm buildings all topped by high thatched roofs. A landscape that told of humankind and earth at peace with one another. It seemed to have been there forever and have no reason to change.

Frau Benzler, a gaunt, stern-looking woman in her fifties, welcomed me with a cup of tea, homemade bread, and honey—in those days, a very friendly and appreciated gesture—and gave me a brief tour of her property. Her impressive compound, which she alone ran, was about three kilometers from town. It comprised her own comfortable living quarters, a small dairy farm, and a dormitory and refectory for about thirty young children and some of their mothers, refugees from the bombarded cities.

Across a spacious yard was the farm of Frau Benzler's enlisted son. Her daughter-in-law, as tall as she but fleshy, blond, and young, was now running the farm.

The weaving shop, a spacious room kept bright and friendly by sky-lights, was located right under the thatched roof of the son's farm-

Fisherman Schulz and his wife

house. Frau Benzler proudly indicated five horizontal looms, each one higher and wider than any I had ever seen.

I said only that I liked the shop. I had fond memories of my grandmother's attic under the thatched roof of her house.

My small white room at Fisherman Schulz's house had a private entrance opening on the flat meadows. There was a vegetable garden on the right and, on the left, the sandy path that led to my workplace half a kilometer away.

A toad spent the whole summer under the wooden floor of my room. Every evening, I waited for the two round, golden notes of its call. Somehow it belonged to the northern summer nights that never get dark.

Fisherman Schulz, a tall, slim man with an easy smile, had lost one eye in the Great War. He did not go fishing any longer but worked at a military hospital a few kilometers away. His young wife had been one of Frau Benzler's weavers. She had come a few years before from her native Austria.

Once the two of us were roaming the beach after a storm, looking for treasures brought by the sea—bits of amber mostly. I asked her whether she was homesick sometimes for her beautiful mountains.

"I have discovered something," she confided. "The sea is as beautiful as the mountains."

She also told me that day that the people who lived by the sea were more refined and friendlier than the mountain people.

Frau Schulz was an accomplished weaver. Her own loom, entirely filling one of the bedrooms in her house, had been built according to her sketches by the local carpenter.

She would permit me to weave two kitchen towels on her loom, but not before I had acquired some skill, months later.

My first days as a salaried weaver were disastrous. I could not handle the big loom.

Of the four other, experienced workers, three were girls in their twenties, and one was a young mother about my age whose six-year-old daughter was in the children's home next door. The young mother's loom faced mine. I looked at her every time I had to retrieve the shuttle that, too often, had jumped down onto the floor. She never showed disapproval or derision. No one else made any remark either. Anyway, we rarely spoke.

Most disturbing to me was the wrong beat at which my loom went—when it went at all. The rhythmic click-click-clack-clack of the other looms sounded right, I knew, without having ever heard a correct beat before.

I don't know how many nine-hour workdays it took before my loom made the proper click-click-clack-clack. But on that day, with French exuberance, I jumped down and applauded myself. The other looms came to a stop, the weavers took time to smile, then resumed work.

Frau Benzler's daughter-in-law lived right under the shop. Would she report when all the looms remained silent for more than a few minutes? We did not know, but she might.

It was, I think, on the third day after my arrival that Frau Benzler managed to get Abel on the phone for me.

We had reassuring words for each other. Everything was fine with me, I said, better, much better, than expected.

Abel was not going to the Atlantic coast in France, as scheduled. It had been discovered that his wife was French. So he was being sent to Russia. Dniepropetrovsk, where the OT was rebuilding the big dam blown up by the Russians. He would go by train. Alone, yes.

"I am going to wear such a drab, ugly, muddy-green uniform, everybody will feel sorry for me rather than be offended by my presence," he said.

Frau Benzler opened a map on her dining-room table.

My husband was going to travel alone, wearing some paramilitary uniform, through more than two thousand kilometers of lands devastated by the Germans: Poland and the Soviet Union. . . .

Frau Benzler understood my anguish. All she could do for me was to say that she wanted me to have tea with her after work.

I thanked her as soberly as I could.

Frau Benzler's farm shortly before it was destroyed, September 1942

I went back to my work, applying all my strength and attention to what I had been hired to do. I was receiving the living wage of a real weaver.

As I toiled at my loom, day after day, I took to remembering Abel at his piano. He would lose contact with our nasty world at the first magic sounds his fingers called to life. And I too was feeling happier, little by little. Or, perhaps, merely gratified when the rhythm of my humble instrument was correct.

I was slow to discover that weaving confers solace.

Why? Because it is such hard work—used to be a man's work—or such good, steady exercise? Or because it is so satisfying to watch one's own creation taking shape, and color, and life under one's own hands?

My days as a weaver were good, warm days in spite of the gray fear that pervaded our lives.

. . .

I had not yet become used to my new surroundings when I received a letter from Hans W.

"Read and burn," it said at the top of the single page.

One week or so before, Hans W.'s friend, whom I had met at dinner, had killed his wife with one of his ominous rapiers. The Gestapo, perhaps called by himself, had burst upon the scene. Hans W.'s friend had screamed accusations and insults at them. They had promptly dispatched him.

Silence. No crimes, no suicides were ever officially reported in this orderly country. Witnesses' whispers alone told about them.

Read and burn.

XXIV

One of the weavers and I were about ten years older than the other workers. We liked to walk, just the two of us, through the meadows or on the beach. Her first name, she told me, was Hilde. I did not know why, but I did not think this was her name.

Her loom faced mine, and we talked about our work. Hilde was weaving tablecloths, only tablecloths, off-white with a beautiful damask pattern. They were sold at the little store that Frau Benzler owned in town.

At the time, one needed coupons to get one meter of cloth—provided one could find a store that had cloth to sell. At Frau Benzler's store in Sankt Peter, Schleswig-Holstein, in the summer of 1942, one could still buy a tablecloth without coupons—or a cloth belt or a tiny cloth purse. One item per person. I don't know how long this luxury lasted.

I told Hilde about my former life in Paris and how I had come to Germany to be with the man I loved.

Hilde volunteered little about herself. She was from Hamburg. Her parents were still there. She was divorced. Recently? Yes, recently.

And we talked about food. Often. The less food one gets, the more one talks about it.

Nobody among the civilian population got much to eat at the time. Not even the farmers. I cannot remember seeing one fat farmer.

The weavers, and an occasional guest, ate at Frau Benzler's table. Still a vegetarian, I did not eat the little bit of meat or fish we sometimes got. I remember potatoes, cabbage, dark mush of some kind, buttermilk, never enough of anything.

Once, when I was taking a walk with Hilde and two other weavers, we came upon a pile of wilted radishes that an old man cleaning his garden had discarded. We ate them, woody, gritty as they were.

I liked Hilde, but something about her disturbed me. She seemed to be afraid, or ashamed of laughing. And she was timid beyond reason. Once, before lunch, we were sitting side by side on the doorsteps in front of Frau Benzler's house when a tall man in the black SS uniform walked down the steps. His high boots nearly touched me. I was startled. Hilde was trembling.

"It's Frau Benzler's son," she told me. "Arrived on furlough last night."

From that day on, she spent most of her free time with her little girl.

Young Herr Benzler, very handsome in his black uniform, paid no attention to any of us. He looked distracted the few times I saw him as he crossed the yard between his farmhouse and his mother's. There was a rumor that mother and son did not get along. Even before he had enlisted, acrimonious discussions had often been overheard by the cook, whose small bedroom was tucked in between the children's dormitory and Frau Benzler's apartment.

The cook, the only fat person in the whole compound, was a warm, friendly girl. She was not much older than the younger weavers, but she was motherly toward them. She saved morsels from the kitchen for them.

"You often have tea with Frau Benzler," she told me.

"Yes," I said.

We smiled.

Nearly every evening after supper, we five weavers took a long walk through the meadows that stretched from Frau Benzler's compound to the eastern horizon. On the west, the meadows stopped at the dunes and the North Sea beyond. We never went toward the thundering sea at night.

Very often, the cook joined us.

There was not much to see on the treeless, deserted meadows at night. The straight, sandy paths that led from one distant farmhouse to another were pale and unmysterious under the light, silky sky and its dimmed stars. We could have revealed secrets only toads, crickets, and such dumb creatures would ever have heard. Yet I kept my thoughts to myself. The others did too. We shared whatever scanty news reached us about recent bombings of cities or the faraway war, victories, mostly. The cook reported local gossip.

"They had a bad exchange last night," the cook reported a week or so after Frau Benzler's son's arrival. "A short one! And I could not understand a word they said, they were so mad at each other. And then, at midnight, a door slammed and after that . . . dead silence."

A few very quiet days passed. Nobody caught sight of young Herr Benzler anywhere. We guessed he had departed the very night he had slammed his mother's door. A whole week before the end of his furlough, he had returned to his unit at the front. To Kharkov? Yes, the cook knew: Kharkov, Russia.

About ten days later, Frau Benzler and her daughter-in-law, both dressed all in black from head to foot, walked side by side, up and down the yard between their two farms. We had never seen them walking together, or even talking.

We knew. An SS soldier had met a hero's death.

XXV

❧

In June, two good letters reached me. One was from Abel, his first.
He had arrived in Saparoscge, near the great river Dnieper and
the big dam of Dniepropetrovsk, Russia, safely—except for a
wound on his ankle inflicted by the beastly boots he had been assigned.
One booted foot, one slippered and bandaged: a most unmilitary pre-
sentation. He loved that, I could tell.

The other letter was from my father. So far, the brief, colorless mis-
sives we had exchanged, Father and I, had said nothing besides, We are
well, we hope you are too, since not one had ever reached us without
having been cut open and soiled with the censor's seal.

For once my father had news he could safely report. My sister's
marriage was going to take place shortly, but, best of all, he had been
nominated secretary of City Hall. Why was he so elated about getting
the demanding, tedious job? I could not have guessed then, but this
was just the job that would permit him to procure food rations and
fake identifications for the resistance fighters.

After my father had retired as a teacher, the family had moved to
my grandparents' house in the beautiful little town of which I had such
happy memories. I loved to imagine them there, where I thought the
German occupation would be uneventful.

The dam at Dniepropetrovsk, Russia, 1942

I hurried to purchase my allotted tablecloth for my sister. Frau Benzler contributed packing paper and string, and I entrusted my modest wedding present to the censors at the post office.

I spent the rainy evenings with Fisherman Schulz and his wife, shared their kitchen table and the light of their kerosene lamp whenever electricity failed.

Fisherman Schulz liked to read poetry to us, often the quiet, wise poems by a poet from Husum, a town on the North Sea about halfway to Hamburg.

One gray Sunday, I took the train there and found the town curiously deserted. People stayed home on Sunday, I decided. Lutherans, reading the Bible?

Cobblestone streets, no restaurant or shop I could identify, townhouses all alike, low and small, looking as if the bright red bricks of their walls and the blue-black slates of their roofs had been freshly scrubbed and shined. And maybe they had.

Russian Woman, *1942* (*watercolor*)

At every undersized window, begonias bearing oversized flowers—glossy red, orange, or yellow—beckoned between parted curtains of stark white lace, improbable, mischievous.

Yes, I believed, one could write poetry in Husum.

This reminded me . . . had I not, and not so long ago, read my own poems in Parisian salons and cafés? As I drifted, uprooted in an alien world, I had forgotten. Forgotten.

More than once I had heard Fisherman Schulz say that his father had been born a Dane, like all his forefathers, for that matter, born before Prussia had grabbed Schleswig-Holstein in 1864.

Because he worked in a hospital, Fisherman Schulz was bound to know more than we did about what was going on in the vast, faraway world. In mid-June, he told us that a great naval battle had recently been fought between Americans and Japanese in the Pacific Ocean. And this time the Americans had won. He could not show us where, all he had was a map of Europe that also showed the Mediterranean Sea and North Africa. He opened the map on the kitchen table. He wanted to show us something, he said. With a weathered finger, he pointed out the countries where German troops were deployed: Norway, Holland, Denmark, Belgium, France, Austria, Czechoslovakia, Yugoslavia, Rumania, Greece, Finland, Poland, a third of Russia . . . the fighting was taking place on a long front in Russia and in the sands of North Africa, all the way from Morocco to Egypt.

Fisherman Schulz wanted us to draw the conclusion. When we did not, he did.

"The Germans are dispersing their forces, losing men every minute that passes, slowly getting weaker and weaker. When they have," he corrected himself, "when we have bled enough, the Americans will come and finish us. Just like in the First World War, but worse."

His young wife was incredulous. She smiled. The German army was mighty strong, she thought. I believed everything he said.

XXVI

W e toiled at our looms nine hours a day, six days a week. The meager food we got kept us slim. But I was getting too slim and too pale. Fisherman Schulz and his wife had, more than once, urged me to pick whatever I liked from their beautiful vegetable garden. I decided to do so. Frau Benzler returned my rations. From then on, I went home for my lunch: a colorful concoction of buttermilk, raw peas, carrots, beans, radishes, parsley, or whatever was in season, plus two slices of my one-kilogram allotment for the week of tough, dark bread.

As a vegetarian, I was entitled to a bit more skim milk and more noodles: one kilogram of gray noodles a month, I seem to remember, instead of the one-half kilogram allotted the meat eaters. I can't remember what I ate for breakfast or supper, but within a few short weeks, I was looking so good that Frau Schulz wondered whether she was not growing miraculous vegetables, as I said she did.

Abel's frequent letters were becoming more cheerful. He was now traveling with a photographer who had a car and a chauffeur and spoke perfect Russian. He wrote about the steppes (the vast Russian grasslands), the Crimea, the Black Sea, Sevastopol, which the Germans had finally taken after a siege of 245 days. He wrote about the Dnieper. He had taken a trip on the great river on a logging raft, and one night there had been a storm, very much like a storm at sea. He already had dozens of sketches. And soon, soon he would be with me.

I had become Frau Benzler's favored weaver. She would let me weave fabric for my own use, and once she gave me precious wool yarn for a sweater. Then one day, at tea, she announced that she wanted me to be the artistic adviser for the shop: I would select the weaving patterns and the yarn colors to be used by the other weavers. She was also raising my salary. Did I deserve this? I was not quite sure, but of course, I was very pleased.

The next morning, I went to work earlier than usual. Hilde was there already. She always was the first at her loom and always took time to greet everybody and smile. That day, Hilde kept her face averted. and the deliberate click-click-clack-clack of her loom was her only greeting. She went on working for over four hours, did not look up once. I caught myself wishing her shuttle would jump out as mine did so that she would have to get down to retrieve it. But Hilde's shuttle never jumped out.

After work, she left the shop in such haste that I did not dare to address her.

The other weavers also had observed the abrupt change in Hilde. "Oh, but we all have our own sorrows," they said. "And anyway, what could we do?"

Two days passed, disturbingly alike.

As I worked, I constantly saw Hilde's sorrowful bent face through the taut thread of our loom's chains. One morning I had a most un-German outburst: I jumped down from my loom. "Hilde, I can't stand it any longer," I shouted. "Say something, please. . . . You make us all feel so bad. How can we help you if we don't know what hurts you?"

All the looms had stopped.

"Sorry . . . I'll tell you," Hilde muttered, "at lunchtime."

She resumed weaving. We all did.

After lunch, Hilde and I walked to the low dunes right behind the beach. We had always favored the nearly deserted area. The low rumble of the sea was enough to smother the sound of our voices. For some reason, we felt that whatever we said had better be kept secret.

That day, Hilde whispered her story rapidly, in chopped, short bursts.

There was a middle-aged farmer who lived close by. He had often had Hilde and her little girl for lunch on Sundays. He was very polite. And then, one day, he had proposed. Hilde had said no. He had invited them again. He had been friendly and a bit sad. Then, one Sunday, Hilde had gone alone. Her little girl had been invited to a picnic. The farmer had served wine. Such a heavy, sweet wine, Hilde could not finish her glass. She had fallen asleep. And the farmer had . . . Hilde could not bring herself to say what the farmer had done. "Now you will have to marry me," he had said. Yes, she knew for sure, she was pregnant.

"Well, then, marry him," I said angrily. How many times had I heard the same sordid story? And yet, I knew how any of us could fall asleep after a glass of wine, underfed as we were.

"Hilde," I said, "you cannot go on weaving those tablecloths forever. Frau Benzler made you weave the whole winter long in that ice-cold attic. Your poor hands are scarred forever by chilblains. What are you going to do with two children? Marry him. . . ."

"I am Jewish," Hilde said quietly.

I had had no idea, Hilde had no idea, in the summer of 1942, of the fate Hitler had reserved for the Jews of Europe. But I knew she was in trouble. I remembered the regulations that had provoked Abel's anger before our marriage. We had had to furnish proof that there had been no Jews among our forebears for four generations!

I also remembered a Jewish young woman married to a German I had known in Stuttgart. We had had the couple over for dinner shortly before our departure. The husband had said, I recalled, that his wife was "protected" because she was married to him, a German.

"Was your husband Jewish?" I asked.

"No."

"Then you were protected by being married. Why did you divorce?"

"He divorced me," Hilde said. "He had to; he would have lost his position."

"His position!" I was outraged. But no matter what I said, Hilde would not utter one word of reproach against her despicable husband.

I helped her perform all the stupid tricks women in her predicament try: jumping down from tables and dressers, running to the point of exhaustion, battling the dangerous surf.

There was a small area of the beach where swimming was permitted and, in theory, possible. But only very strong and experienced swimmers ventured beyond the treacherous surf. The Nord See was called the Mord See in the area.

I persuaded Hilde to go with me there. She could not swim and was scared of only stepping into the wild water. In her despair, she let the murderous waves tumble her, nearly drown her. The waves tumbled me too. But I knew how and when to dive under them and when not to breathe. Hilde did not.

Nothing worked. Precious time passed.

Asking Frau Benzler for help and, of course, telling her everything was the last recourse. Hilde said she could not bring herself to do it, she was too ashamed.

But she must have, even sooner than I thought. One day she told us that she was taking one week off to visit her parents. Early the following morning, I saw her walking toward the railroad station with Frau Benzler's daughter-in-law. Each carried a small suitcase. In the light fog of an August morning, two silhouettes—the all-in-black tall widow of an SS soldier towering above the little Jewish woman by her side.

XXVII

❧

A wave of optimism washed over Germany in the middle of August when the *Führer* announced that our victorious armies had captured the Maikop oil fields in the Caucasus.

"Might be a bit late for General Rommel," Fisherman Schulz commented. And he went on to explain that Rommel, the glorious conqueror of North Africa, had begun to lose ground. Why? No fuel for his tanks.

Our newspapers had no room for such information since they had so many victories and sinkings of enemy vessels to report.

Where could one get such an interesting piece of news? Radio? England was only eight hundred kilometers away, and the BBC . . . It was *verboten*—under pain of death—to listen to the BBC.

Fisherman Schulz never said what his source of information was. Frau Benzler too was rigidly, painfully discreet. She mentioned victories, never commented. Never uttered any criticism either. She sheltered Hilde, and probably others. I never tried to find out. Everybody knew it was better not to know.

. . .

One morning, Hilde, back from her vacation, sat at her loom. She was a bit pale, perhaps, but she smiled. After lunch, we took a walk on the beach. Frau Benzler and her daughter-in-law had been so good to her, she said. She was fine now. Thanks to them, she insisted, and yes, she had seen her parents. They had abandoned their large apartment in the center of town and had moved to a very small place.

Hilde did not volunteer more. I asked no questions. She had told me enough already. I hoped she knew I could keep a secret. We never spoke about it.

On the eighteenth of August, another victory I mourned was announced. A thousand Canadian commandos had been wiped out in Dieppe, a French fishing harbor on the channel. I had spent a vacation there when a small child. Everything, I remembered, had been gray: the sky, the beach pebbles hard under my naked feet, and the waves busy churning and polishing the pebbles. A gray tomb for the Canadian commandos.

There was something I was grateful for in my present primitive life: the absence of a radio at Fisherman Schulz's house. If there was one at Frau Benzler's compound, I never heard it. I never had to listen to bragging, loud *Sonder Meldungs* as I had on the streets of Stuttgart.

On August 22, the German armies reached Stalingrad, a city of half a million inhabitants in the southeast of Russia, on the Volga. The *Führer's* goal. Another great victory.

Fisherman Schulz shook his head as he read the newspaper.

Beggar, Russia, 1942 *(charcoal)*

"The southeast of Russia is not the Riviera," he said. "Stalingrad must be at about the latitude of Vienna. General Winter will be there soon."

A letter from Abel brought good news: he was on his way, would deliver a heavy load of drawings to the OT headquarters in Berlin, and expected to be rewarded with a long vacation.

XXVIII

❦

Abel arrived in Sankt Peter at the beginning of September, about the time the German army broke through to the Volga, south of Stalingrad. Another great victory.

The picture Abel presented in his shabby uniform and house slippers was not in harmony with the mood of the day. The sore on his ankle had worsened—field hospitals were run by the military and would not treat OT *Bildberichterstatters*. The military would not feed them either. The army and the OT were, one could say, "friendly enemies."

Two of Abel's fingers had become infected from carrying a crudely made piece of wooden luggage containing treasures from the Ukraine: honey and sunflower oil.

But worst of all was the memory of how the drawings he had been so proud of had been received by the officials at OT headquarters in Berlin.

"You have been hired to do propaganda for the OT, not for Russia!"

Indeed, who wanted to know how Russian women and their ramshackle houses looked, or beggars and their babies wrapped up in newspapers, or the Dnieper and its storms, or the soldiers looting in Sebastopol?

"Looting? Our soldiers do not loot!"

Tempest on the Dniepr, *1942* (*charcoal*)

"Romanian soldiers," Abel had explained.

"Under German command!"

I saw a rough sketch of the surrealistic drawing: smoking ruins as a background for soldiers carrying off grandfather clocks on their shoulders.

In the end, Abel's drawings had been shelved and he had been told once more what was expected from him. His contract, to his surprise, had been renewed. He had been sent home to get his ankle well and await a new assignment.

There had been a sinister last note to Abel's Russian adventure: the body of the photographer with whom he had traveled to out-of-the-way places for the past three months had been found in his own car, cut into small pieces. Signature of the Russian underground.

Newspapers had described at length how German soldiers had been received with dances and flowers by the Russian people they had liberated from Stalin's tyranny; they never mentioned the underground.

I counted on my ministrations and Sankt Peter's calm, sun, and sea for the healing of all Abel's wounds.

First, the infected fingers. I boiled my nail scissors and cut out the dead skin, exactly as our village pharmacist had done to my infected hand when I was five years old. Then I drenched the skinned fingers with iodine—that was all we had—and let the sun do the rest. It worked. The ankle's sores were another matter. My diligent applications of wet dressings and iodine, sun and sea bathing, made them worse. We decided to count on time and neglect.

Meanwhile, Frau Benzler was trying to persuade us to stay in Sankt Peter, a much safer place than the big city.

"You remember what happened to Cologne," she said.

Cologne had been devastated on the last day of May by British planes—in just a single night.

"Well, we started it," Frau Benzler said with a thin, bitter smile.

"I'll find a house for you," she promised.

But Abel had to go back to Stuttgart. He was supposed to be waiting there for a new assignment. And then, he wanted to see to it that his mother went to stay with one of her daughters who lived in a small town.

The cool summer was turning into a cooler fall. The nights were still clear and beautiful. Crickets were still chirping, toads still sending out tuneful calls.

We said our good-byes, Frau Benzler said she hoped we would come back. I asked Fisherman Schulz and his wife to promise me that they would provide help to Hilde and her little girl in case something unforeseen happened. They smiled brightly—knowingly, perhaps—and promised.

I was sad the morning we left. Sankt Peter was all wrapped up in a kind, light mist, as everything had been there, gray-green landscape, faraway rumbling sea, silent nights, people's calm ways, and even Hilde's tragic story.

Why were we returning to *Sonder Meldungs*, strutting uniforms, and murderous nights? We could have moved to Sankt Peter if we had wanted to.

O n the train, people spoke of trains being shot at by low-flying planes. Someone knew a young woman who had had her right arm shattered by a bullet as she sat at the compartment's window one morning on her way to work.

We stopped in Hamburg to visit Hans W. and his wife. They were still traumatized by their friends' strange and tragic demise.

Hans predicted Hamburg would meet Cologne's fate.

We all waved and smiled bravely as we parted. Every good-bye might be the last one.

XXIX

❧

Stuttgart, October 1942. Everybody there was working hard and feeling good about it. As if work were an end in itself. Trees on the hills above the city, along the avenues, in parks and deserted beer gardens displayed festive reds and yellows. There had been some air raids but, so far, little visible damage.

The sirens wailed one night shortly after our return. We got dressed and walked down to the cellar, as orderly citizens were expected to do.

The shallow cellar under our three-story house was divided into three cubicles by partitions made of unpainted narrow wooden slats. The cubicles of the slim, blond widow and the lawyer were furnished with tables, chairs, and shelves sagging under rows of red and green jars of preserves. By the smell, we guessed potatoes and cabbage stacked somewhere. Our cubicle, the smallest, was bare and dusty. Abel and I sat on crates abandoned there by the former tenant.

Where were the lawyer's housekeeper and the widow's two young Italian maids? Was there a cubicle for servants? Where?

We tried not to stare through the slats at our neighbors. Anyway, we were all caged and scared.

We had exchanged subdued greetings. Now we listened to the

crepitations of our antiaircraft guns and the contralto of bombs falling. In the distance, not on our city. We all guessed that the factories in the industrial suburbs were keeping death away from us. Relieved, we took deep gulps of foul underground air. When the all clear sounded, briskly stepping out of our cubicles and climbing the few steep steps out of our shelter cellar, we wished one another a smug *"Gute Nacht."*

"Let's stay upstairs next time," Abel said. "I could at least play the piano."

So next time, we stayed in our apartment.

We stood at the opened window, searching the clear night.

Suddenly, out of nowhere, there were two black toy-like airplanes among the stars. They dived down into the dark valley where the town was.

Deafening explosion. We lost track of things, got lifted up and deposited back, in one swoop—or so it seemed—wobbly, giggling like children on a trampoline.

We looked around. The piano was whole. Nothing had moved.

"Der Bahnhof!" Abel said.

We ran down the stairs, met no one, walked out into the street. The railroad station, *der Bahnhof,* was located right at the bottom of the hill on which our house stood. Trees and houses built on the slopes, we knew, obstructed the view. We peered into the darkness anyway. There was nothing to see. No fire. No smoke. No one. Dead silence. As if nothing had happened.

We went back to our apartment, slept. If any fire truck or ambulance drove by, we did not hear it. At dawn we walked down toward the winding road with the trolley line leading downtown. We took the shortcut—part steep path, part narrow brick stairs—that led almost straight down between vegetable gardens and fruit trees to the railroad station at the center of town.

We had always favored the shortcut. We had taken it one rainy May morning, going to City Hall to get married. We had had a curious exchange then.

"I never wanted to marry you," I had said.

"Me neither," Abel had said.

Then we had laughed. True, we had wanted no ties. Our marriage, at that moment, appeared more like a prank played on ourselves.

A few minutes later we had been in front of the dark City Hall, ominous flags waving, our two witnesses waiting for us. Both wore the party badges. A prank, or a bad dream?

Nearly three years had passed.

The plaza in front of the railroad station was deserted.

In the dim light of dawn, the tall building looked whole. Doors were all wide open. That was odd. We walked in. The high, vaulted ceiling over the lofty main hall was gone. The white sky rested on top of the high walls. There was an uncanny absence of rubble.

Abel looked up. "Much better that way. Much, much better. At last I can breathe."

I looked up at Abel. How could he have been oppressed by a vaulted ceiling as high as a cathedral's?

He was taking deep gulps of cold air and smiling.

Doors, gates, windows blown away. Neatly. We walked through.

Aghast, we stood on the platform. An infantile giant had jumbled up his toy trains. Not broken or squashed them. Intact carriages ran sideways, backward, lay toppled over on their heads, their wheels riding the air. One—long, slender, brand new, green—was mounting a crouching velvety-black locomotive. Rails agleam forced up into unfinished question marks.

No sign of life. Or death. Silence. Had all those carriages been empty of passengers? We did not want to know. We walked out. An older gentleman in his ample loden coat, green felt hat, cane in hand, crossed the majestic main hall now opened to a bright morning sky—the lone ghost of a gone Germany. He did not acknowledge our presence.

In the paper, the event was minimized. No death was mentioned. Crews of workers would toil day and night. Soon trains would be running. On time.

Life went on.

Abel consulted Dr. Müller. The sores on his ankle had been spreading.

"Ulcers," Dr. Müller diagnosed. He cauterized the large sore and the small ones around it. They finally healed.

Dr. Müller, as optimistic as ever, Abel said, predicted victory.

So did the dentist I had to consult. I knew him and I disliked him, but he was the only one available.

On his waiting-room walls, the newspaper clippings picturing Poles torturing elderly Germans had been replaced by clippings of Russian maidens greeting their German liberators with big bunches of flowers.

The dentist recounted for my benefit and the nurse's all the conquests the *Führer* had made—in record time. And now, he was telling us, the Mediterranean Sea was a German-Italian sea, France was our friend, and Russia was finished.

Then the dentist heard from the nurse that I was a vegetarian. "Like our *Führer!*" he cried out.

I swore to myself that I would eat the first chunk of meat that came my way. It did not happen for nearly two years.

Meanwhile, the dentist assured me that since only one root of my three-root molar was bad, he could extract the bad root and put a crown on the remaining good part of the tooth.

He split the tooth, cracking my jaw in the process, and extracted the bad root. The painful procedure was not a success.

B y chance, on the street one day, we met a lawyer Abel had known when he was working at the advertising agency, a wiry, resolute, thin-lipped man, his eyes gleaming behind thick lenses. He said he was in a hurry but felt he had to brief us about the all-around optimistic picture. In clipped words barely audible to a chance passerby, he announced that *Ivan* (the Russians) was about to surround the sixth (the German Sixth Army), yellow friends (the Japanese) had lost a big ship, and the British were poised to cut our African army to pieces while Rommel was sick at home.

"*Viel Glück*," the lawyer shouted as he hurried away.

A bel had been unable to convince his mother to leave the city.
"And who would take care of my grandson?" she had asked.

Younger brother had, seven years before, married a young woman who had worked in an office. It had been convenient then for the new couple and for the lonely old mother to stay together in her fairly large apartment. She had been happy later on to raise their child.

Now that the father was enlisted, the mother working, she was needed more than ever.

Abel's mother, we knew even if she did not tell us, was wondering why we had not presented her yet with another grandchild.

How could we tell her that we had resolved not to have children as long as the Nazis were in power?

The order of the day was to have children, many children, for "our

Führer." Which should be enough, Abel said, to prevent any reasonable human being from conceiving.

Abel's mother did not know, did not understand, would never understand—or believe—what the Nazi regime was.

One day I got into a conversation with the beautician in a fashionable store on Main Street. She was French.

"This is my last day here," she said. "Tomorrow I'll be a factory worker."

In a helpless gesture, she opened her soft white hands.

Three months before, in France, she had been contracted as a beautician for the store—travel expenses paid. Suddenly her position had been eliminated, and she had been pressured into accepting work in an ammunition factory.

"No money for my return ticket," she said.

With revulsion, I imagined myself turning out bullets used to kill Germany's enemies—my friends. I did not know at the time that the Germans were executing hostages in France—daily.

Abel and I approached the editor of a publishing house for whom Abel had previously illustrated some books.

As a matter of fact, yes, the editor knew of a book, a thick book, that, he thought, would have to be translated into French sometime. He gave me a letter of intent—contract pending.

Abel played Mozart that evening. He played Mozart whenever he recognized the intervention of his guardian angel.

At the end of October, he received his new assignment in Finland. Finland in November, a dark month. Abel departed for Berlin, where he would be given his itinerary and, he hoped, a warmer uniform.

A letter arrived from Fisherman Schulz.

Two weeks after we had left Sankt Peter, on a beautiful, clear night,

British planes had dropped firebombs on all the big farms in the area. Thatched roofs, houses, and barns had all gone up in flames. Frau Benzler's compound had burned to the ground. Scattered little houses had been spared.

"Our house has not suffered any damage. We are both in good health. Hilde and her little girl have come to live with us. We all remember you fondly. We hope you are well."

X X X

❧

This slice of life, fifty years in the past, is a tragicomic mural on the walls of a cave. My memory, like a flashlight, its batteries half spent, conjures stray images out of the darkness. Some jump out whole, as immediate as life itself, others appear mangled and almost foreign, others don't show up at all.

In November 1942, Hitler sent his armies into unoccupied France; British and American forces beat German forces in North Africa while Russian forces encircled the mighty German army before Stalingrad. All I remember from this fateful month is waiting for the letter that would tell me to join Abel in Berlin, trying to make new clothes out of old ones, and spending a dismal afternoon with younger brother's six-year-old boy while his grandmother had gone to the doctor.

The boy was tall and heavy for his age, and I too small to impress him. He kept mimicking every one of my words and snickering. He knew only *Schwäbisch*, the local dialect, and I spoke *hoch Deutsch* (high German). He thought I was showing off.

Abel's few letters told little. The days were too short, the nights too long, and there was no landscape, he wrote, just snow, swamps, and cold mist. Then suddenly he was back in Berlin and expecting me.

From some acquaintance, I had gotten the address of an opera singer who lived in a Berlin suburb and was willing to rent one room to me.

I don't know how I reached the railway station with my two heavy suitcases. No help or taxi was available, and trolleys stopped running early. I know I boarded a late-night train. From then on, I remember every detail.

In the compartment I picked were three tall, ponderous gentlemen wearing black business suits. Well-fed gun makers, I decided. Or bankers. They rushed to help me with my cumbersome luggage. Polite and reserved, they did not spare little bows and *gnädige Frau* (gracious lady) but were, I guessed, rather put out by my presence.

I curled up in my upholstered corner and went to sleep. I woke up hours later, uncurled, stretched, combed my short hair with my fingers, and smiled. Red-rimmed eyes peered at me out of white, bloated faces as if I belonged to a different species. I enjoyed that.

"Ich habe sehr gut geschlafen!" I told them in my best French-accented German. I did not ask whether they had slept well. Their black suits were horribly wrinkled.

In Berlin, the platform was crowded with soldiers and civilians. I soon spotted Abel. He was pale and emaciated, and I wondered why I had brought so many clothes, shoes, and hats.

We pulled and pushed my suitcases in and out of subway trains and subway stations, up and down stairs, on a sandy path through pine woods, and finally along the sidewalks of a suburban street. Three-story houses on each side, tall apartment buildings here and there. No traces of bombing so far.

The opera singer had a large apartment in one of the three-story houses. We had heard her sing the part of a Walkyrie at Stuttgart's opera house.

Still a Walkyrie, I thought as she greeted us in a loud voice. She was not tall, and her hair was too dark for the part, but she had powerful shoulders, a harshly cut mouth, a strong nose, wide-set steel-gray eyes, and a bold, almost uncouth way of addressing people.

She offered me a large, unheated room in which half of a wide bed was encumbered with boxes, luggage, and equipment of some kind. I recognized a sunlamp. It took me a few days to understand that the Walkyrie had offered me a place to sleep only because she had wanted a French nanny for her two-year-old son instead of the German one she had. Extricating myself from the situation without losing the use of my half-bed was not easy.

Abel was quartered in a hotel downtown to await orders. He shared a room with another OT man. We saw each other in cafés where a strange, dark brew called coffee was served. We searched for restaurants where we ate very light meals. We took long walks. The air was cool, dry, and pure. There were few cars, no crowded sidewalks, except for lines of quiet women and old men in front of rare stores or rarer restaurants. People walked fast and kept to themselves.

The artwork Abel had brought back from Finland had been well received by OT officials.

"That assignment was a punishment," Abel said. "To begin with, I froze in the little canvas coat lined with flimsy rabbit fur I was allocated. The big, ugly new boots fitted. But the contraption I needed to pull them off was stolen, and to construct a new one, I had to destroy the only chair in the room!"

To get food, lodging, transportation, and—most important—what Abel had to represent had been frustrating chores. The OT camps were scattered over a thousand kilometers of forest, lakes, and swamps from the Baltic Sea to Murmansk, the last northern outpost on the frozen Barents Sea.

"In Murmansk, I met men in their twenties who were losing their

Finland, 1942

teeth," Abel said, "posted too long, forgotten up there. . . . As for those poor, freezing, hungry, bored German and Russian soldiers, their only pastime was shooting at each other. But only occasionally! Short on ammunition on both sides? I wondered. No bullet was wasted on me when I sketched these fancy bunker igloos."

The only solace had been meeting the rightful inhabitants of the land, the short, big-headed Laplanders who waited placidly for the white man's murderous antics to cease. Abel had wondered at their patient smiles and strong teeth, at their odd customs, like putting salt and sugar into their coffee.

"Real coffee! Where, how did they get it? Lapland, the only place I ever got a cup of honest coffee!"

The day Abel was ready to leave, an epidemic of typhus broke out.

Murmansk, Finland, 1942

"A high wood fence went up overnight, and access to Helsinki was blocked. The quarantine could last for weeks ... months! And I was strongly advised not to try to jump over the fence, punishment could be severe."

On the following night, Abel threw his backpack containing all his precious drawings over the fence and climbed, jumped, crawled, rolled down after it.

"They forgot to post a sentinel, I guess," he said.

In Helsinki, by chance, Abel met a military pilot who was about to fly an old Junkers plane back to Berlin and, with a bottle of aqua vitae, bought a scary, uncomfortable ride.

The old plane flew at a low altitude. Abel spotted, among ice floes, small boats equipped with guns.

"Good imitation," the pilot said, laughing. "Fishing boats equipped with tree trunks! Not enough guns to patrol the Baltic these days."

. . .

Weeks later, rummaging through Abel's messy backpack, I found, wrapped in sketching paper and socks, the small, fragile wood carving of a bird with wings spread.

"A present," Abel said. "Well, I took it as a present. Found it on a log in the woods. At this OT camp where I was stationed for a while. Oh, well, I had left a chunk of bread on that log every day at noon. A Russian prisoner was working alone there. All these poor devils got for food was the camp's garbage. . . ."

The Russian carving would join the photograph and the matchbox, Abel's Spanish coprisoners' ultimate presents. Sentimental tokens or charms, they would go with us wherever we went during the forty-year peregrination that was in our future—we moved thirty times and abandoned our furniture three times. It was not so long ago that I burned a wingless and tailless bird carving and a crushed matchbox. I still have the photograph.

XXXI

❦

Berlin was the worst of Germany, Abel told me: Prussian.
But I rather liked the city. This was not the utterly cold
foreign town I had expected. On some streets, the neat rows
of houses reminded me of my own country. Eighteenth-century French
architecture! I remembered my history book: in 1685, French Hugue-
nots had been banished by Louis XIV, 400,000 of them. Most had emigrated to friendly Lutheran Germany and built those French-looking
German houses.

My first impression of the people was not unfavorable either. They
seemed to have a dry wit I could enjoy.

"Pretentious and overbearing," Abel said.

Once in the course of one of our walks through the city, we happened to be standing on the sidewalk opposite the Reichskanzlei
(Chancellery) at the moment when Goering and his military attendants walked down the steps, then crossed toward their parked cars.
For a moment, we found ourselves less than three meters from the
smiling, self-satisfied field marshal. He carried his baton. His cheeks
were plump, rosy, and smooth. He wore makeup, I swear. His leather
greatcoat of a subtle gray-green color nearly hid fine matching boots.

He eased his heavy bulk into a long automobile of the same subtle gray-green.

I was highly entertained by the spectacle. Abel was not. For days, weeks, he was obsessed by having been close enough to the "sinister clown" to kill him.

Our evenings were spent searching for a café or a restaurant where we could get something to eat or drink. Anything. Once, in a café on Kurfürstendamm, we got French wine. It had spoiled. We drank it anyway. We got sick, of course. We did not care.

Often we found nothing.

Late in the evening, Abel would accompany me to the Walkyrie's apartment, then run back to catch the last subway train.

Once the sirens sounded early, and Abel could not leave. With other people, we spent part of the night in an open garage. The suburban houses, built on sandy soil, had no cellars. The opera singer was in town. I don't know where her little boy and his nanny were.

We listened to the chattering of the flaks, looked up at the fiery streaks they made on the night sky. Bombs fell. Not far away. The earth shook. I kept shivering. From fear or from cold? Anyway, we finished a box of chocolate candy, our Christmas ration.

Abel shared my half bed for the rest of the night. Since his shaving kit was in his hotel room downtown, we left very early.

The suburban streets were deserted, the predawn air chilly. No traces of the previous night's bombing. We wondered. But then, suddenly, there it was, close to the street, a deep, clean crater where only yesterday a seven-story apartment building had been. This did not seem possible.

We walked on. What else could we do?

We both had the same thought. "At least it went fast."

"In just a little while," Abel predicted, "we will become as sensitive as ants."

The next evening, when Abel accompanied me back, the Walkyrie pompously reproached him for having spent the night in her house.

"No matter what, you should have rejoined your quarters," she said.

Abel chose to laugh.

Long days passed, cold and lean, truncated nights too, and the dead hours spent in cellars or public shelters wherever we happened to be when sirens sounded. All so utterly carefree, it felt almost like happiness—and maybe it was happiness.

"The OT officials have forgotten all about me," Abel said.

Foolishly, we rejoiced.

But then one day, he was informed by letter that he would have to present himself at OT headquarters in the first week of January. We rushed back to Stuttgart, checked on the elderly mother, picked up our skis and sports clothes, weathered the blond widow's reproaches for neglecting our duties as tenants, and boarded the first train for Sankt Anton, Austria, Abel's favorite resort.

He did not even open his piano.

XXXII

❦

D ecember 24, 1942, Sankt Anton am Arlberg, Austria. For one whole week under the protection of the virgin mountains, crawling like crazed pilgrims up icy slopes for the brief ecstasies of a few mad spins, pretending that we had never known the bombs' hiss of death, the walls crashing down in the night, the cellar-shelters stinking of angst and rotten potatoes.

"I made reservations for Christmas-night supper at the *gasthaus*," Abel said.

I shrugged.

"Wine—somebody said there will be wine."

The doors to the *gasthaus's* lofty dining room opened at 10 P.M. exactly. We filed in, in an orderly manner: yesteryear's long dresses, mothballed tuxedos, fur-lined military greatcoats, and, thanks to the war, shabby ski outfits like ours. A laughable parade. Nobody laughed.

Dark beams had sprouted evergreens; a jolly Christmas tree stood watch in the eastern corner; chandeliers shed poor but kind light; flowery drapes nearly concealed the black paper shades that blinded the windows; crystal, silver, and china brimmed with promises on starched white tablecloths.

With stiff little bows, we introduced ourselves, my French accent unnoticed, I hoped, sat down, nine at every one of a dozen massive round tables. Half a century of pipe and cigar smoke embedded in the ancient wood paneling provided sly intoxication. A Christmas carol drifted thinly from a radio.

Waitresses in cheerful dirndls proceeded to serve the festive meal. Holding knives and forks in fastidious hands, eschewing vulgar haste, we dined on three slices of red beets, bizarre gray meat sopping up pale gravy, and—blessed be Austria—cauliflower, not rutabaga. Wine, yes, there was wine, two glasses per guest. Voices grew louder and tobacco smoke billowed overhead. One gets drunk cheaply during lean years.

Hush! Religious silence required: Goebbels's Christmas message had supplanted the Christmas song.

A young man at our table silently got to his feet. He had previously introduced himself as a dentist. The tuxedo hung loose on his thin frame. With a magician's gestures he borrowed a brooch from the lady seated near him, showed around its long golden pin, and put it into his mouth. The pin went through his cheek, stuck out right in the middle of it, causing no flow of blood or, apparently, pain. The dentist extracted the pin from his cheek and, smiling, offered the brooch to every one of us in turn.

"Doesn't hurt," he mouthed his words. "Try . . . try."

We cringed. He repeated the operation on his other cheek.

On the radio, Goebbels's vociferation mixed with raucous static.

"It has all happened before," a man facing me at the table said. Blue suit, puffed face, shiny eyes. He had not bothered to lower his voice.

"Our brave soldiers shall crush the barbarian hordes bent on destroying the civilized world," Goebbels announced.

"Civilized world? Where, where is that?" Abel asked.

The dentist, mouthing exaggerated thanks, returned the borrowed brooch to its owner.

"It's all in the Bible," the man in the blue suit said, and pointed a shaking finger at the radio. "The beast that spews fire and smoke . . . Remember? Remember?"

A sudden clatter at a faraway table made heads turn. A gray-haired man had gotten to his feet and pushed back his heavy chair. Stalking around tables, he crossed the whole length of the dining room, lunged for the radio, turned it off. Dead silence. All eyes followed the man as he stiffly walked back to his seat, his face flushed. He sat down. The whole room burst into a song.

O Tannenbaum, O Tannenbaum,
Wie grün sind deine Blättern . . .

Everybody sang, I sang, the man in the blue suit sang, ruddy-faced men in uniform sang. We finished the song and started all over, the same song.

At half past midnight, as if on a secret signal, we stopped singing, got to our feet and, with stiff little bows, mumbled" *Glückliches Weihnachten*" and walked out into the cold. Except for ladies in long dresses, men in tuxedos and military greatcoats, who remained in the *gasthaus.*

Abel and I were staying at a farmhouse a half kilometer or so away. Digging our own path with slow feet, we trudged through the village. Squatty one-story houses crouched, animal and remote, under their white furs. Too smug, we said. The church steeple, a toy, pricked at the black velvet sky. A thousand stars danced. We stumbled and laughed, drunk on a bit of wine, old hunger, and thin air.

We left the village. Slowly. We had all the time in the world. The snowy valley stretched in front of us, steeped in a light of its own, silent and foreign. We marveled at how foreign everything was. The hamlet we were heading for was a black blotch. Far away. We did not mind, we were not tired. We shivered and said we were not cold. We discovered a dark dot staggering on the invisible path. The dot grew bigger. It struggled toward us. It took human shape. In the vast white night, we were going to meet a stranger and, by luck, right at the crossroad where a tiny shrine to Sankt Anthony was perched on a low post, snow heaped high on its narrow wooden roof.

"*Glückliches Weihnachten!*"

"*Glückliches Weihnachten!*"

"*Glückliches Weihnachten!*"

He was a soldier. And he was very young. He too shivered in his shabby uniform. No fur-lined greatcoat for him.

The Russian front. He told us about the Russian front.

"On my way back there, on my way." He shrugged.

Drunk too.

Holding on to one another's shoulders, to placate the demons that feed on the souls of slaves, I guess, we bawled, once more, the same childish "*O Tannenbaum.*"

XXXIII

Back in Berlin, out of a dream and into another dream. Abel's new assignment, baffling and welcomed, consisted of illustrating books. Books intended for OT workers busy building fortifications, dams, bridges, roads and more roads from the French beaches to the Russian steppes. Good books too. Germany's ancient history and some world literature: *Tom Sawyer, Huckleberry Finn.*

I was stunned. Maybe I had not understood what the OT was.

"Dr. Todt," Abel explained once more, "the engineer who built the great German highways and who during the war became Minister of Armaments, created the Organization Todt for the building of fortifications on the Atlantic coast and roads in the occupied territories. Then, when Dr. Todt was killed in a strange plane explosion, Hitler's favored architect, Albert Speer, had become minister of armaments and head of the OT."

Interesting, but I still did not understand the new literary endeavor.

"In the Third Reich, miracles happen daily," Abel said. "A wine salesman becomes the minister of foreign affairs, a fighter pilot becomes the overseer of the entire economy, an architect becomes minister of armaments, road builders become book publishers."

We left the Walkyrie and went to live in the apartment of the house *Wächter*.

Wächters were middle-aged men who kept order in and around apartment houses, watched that no streak of light showed at any window at night, herded tenants to cellars or garages in case of air raids. They might have had other functions too.

This *Wächter* took pity on us, maybe. He offered us his teenaged daughters' bedroom, and we gladly accepted.

A nice, orderly bedroom with a big window. Unheated. Abel stayed in bed, wore gloves with their fingertips snipped off to draw illustrations for *Tom Sawyer*. I searched for food, stood in line for one potato or two, a chunk of rutabaga or cabbage, and cooked them on the *Wächter's* coal-burning kitchen stove.

Wife and daughters were polite and uncommunicative, but the *Wächter* liked to chat. Once we met him in the entrance hall of the house and told him about something freakish we had seen while walking through streets bombed the night before: in a gutted building, a single electric bulb dangling from a beam, still lit.

The *Wächter* ranted loudly—so as to be heard by every tenant—against unpatriotic people who left their lights on during air raids. Should be reported . . . arrested . . .

"Dead or alive," Abel said evenly.

The *Wächter* ranted some more, then abruptly stopped. Never chatted with us again.

On Kurfürstendamm, there was still a bit of night life. The cafés at times would fill up with soldiers. Young, boisterous, drunk on their own noise, mostly. Mere boys propped up by their uniforms, Abel said. We avoided them. They did not care much for civilians anyway.

We met other artists employed by the OT, befriended one, a melancholy man with prematurely gray hair. He told us about the tapestry-weaving shop he owned in the suburbs of Lübeck. His wife and teenaged daughter still lived there.

Lübeck's inner city, a medieval jewel on the Baltic Sea, had been devastated in a single night by savage bombings. The drab suburbs had been spared.

The melancholy artist one evening made a strange request: Would I, please, go visit his wife and try to persuade her not to divorce him?

"I don't know what has happened to her mind," he said. "She is Jewish. Do you understand what divorcing would mean for her?"

Yes, I said, I understood.

I could not refuse the request. My visit was easily arranged since I was a weaver eager to see beautiful tapestries.

I took the train for Lübeck, not without misgivings.

A tall, tastefully dressed, proud woman in her forties met me at the railway station. She had beautiful emerald eyes. She was the perfect hostess. I tried to be the best possible guest. We spent one week together, talking easily, like people who share a common sorrow.

She was a professional violinist, forbidden to perform because of her race. She submitted to her unjust fate, not with the humility that had so irritated me in Hilde but with a frightening pride.

"Our marriage began to deteriorate when our daughter was diagnosed with mental retardation. A terrible blow to my husband's ego," she said. "I am tired of it all, I want a divorce!"

I had observed the girl. She was not beautiful like her mother. A plain, sweet, docile blond of fourteen, she was learning to weave. Slowly.

"How could a divorce remedy such a problem?" I impulsively asked and got no answer.

. . .

We stumbled along ancient Lübeck's torn-up streets, between oddly clean mounds of fine-grained ceramic bricks where houses had once stood. One, sample and witness, was still erect. Five stories tall, of a quiet red hue toned by the centuries—gutted, its windows agape and dark. Over it all was an unbearable silence one did not dare to disturb.

Warily we stepped over the mutilated threshold of a church. Steeple and vaulted roof gone, stained-glass windows blown away, buttressed walls still standing as well as a precarious, thin arch above the entrance. The great organ had melted down into a cascade of verdigris over the high altar, an abstract sculpture now with its own cryptic beauty and message of doom.

"Johann Sebastian Bach played on this organ," my companion said, her voice lowered to a whisper.

Like awed worshippers, we stood in the cold skeleton of the church, unable, unwilling to detach our eyes from the barbaric new icon that crushed the high altar.

"Illiterate" American Negro pilots had thrown the bombs down on Lübeck, the gullible German public had been told.

My proud hostess never wore the armband with the yellow star that all Jews had been ordered to wear in public. She knew how dangerous it was to disobey such an order. She wanted, I by now understood, to provoke fate. Divorcing would only be a worse provocation. This was madness, of course. But was not madness stalking the streets of the doomed cities? Abel too was mad, I often thought.

"I understand you," I said shortly before I departed. "Oh, I understand you. . . ." And the sullen stare in the emerald eyes gave way to surprise.

Having nothing better to offer, I humbly passed on to her what a young artist in Stuttgart had once told me and I, so often, had whispered to myself like a spell.

"All the demons are on the loose right now. Don't listen to them. Lie low and wait. Demons do not last."

Many years later, when Abel and I were living in New York, a German friend of friends of the bad old days paid us a visit. In the course of the conversation, we inquired about this couple from Lübeck.

"He became a professor in a university! Oh, but we rather shun him. He wanted to divorce his Jewish wife during the war, did you know that?"

So many errors are never corrected.

XXXIV

On January 31, 1943, Abel and I sat in a café on Kurfürstendamm with people I have now forgotten, except one: the
Walkyrie. Her face under a vast blue felt hat offered a
tragic mask. On that day, General Friedrich Paulus, promoted to field
marshal only twenty-four hours before, had surrendered to the Russians at Stalingrad and with him 90,000 exhausted survivors out of an
army of 300,000. The defeat had not been officially conceded, but
everybody knew.

Many people, civilians and soldiers, had gathered in the café that
night. There was nothing to drink or eat, and no one could exchange
two honest words or dare to rejoice. Neither the outspoken patriot—
the *Führer* had not yet set the tone—nor the others who hoped,
wished, prayed they were witnessing the beginning of the end.

But then there was the Walkyrie. At some point, she directed her
eyes toward the smudged ceiling.

"Think, oh think of all the angels flying to heaven tonight," she de-
claimed, her face suddenly radiant.

Some heads turned.

Abel and I soon took our leave.

This was the last time we saw the Walkyrie. Two days later, our landlord-*Wächter* advised us through his wife that it was time for us to vacate their daughters' bedroom.

Abel explained at OT headquarters that he would draw better and faster in his own home, where he had space to work and art supplies at hand. The OT employee in charge understood and sent him home to illustrate books while waiting for a new assignment abroad.

"Something interesting," Abel said. "I have so far not met one good, genuine Nazi at the OT."

Abel and his piano were reunited. And once more, we forgot the nasty world that was out there waiting for us. I never tried to understand why the music Abel made had such power over me as well as over him. There was a noble fluidity in his play, a respect for every note, a deliberate avoidance of fortissimos and pianissimos that I recognized and loved. And also something sustaining, exhilarating I did not care to explain. I could no more analyze than make music. I read it well enough to turn pages for the pianist, humbly, joyfully.

A t the time, there was a rumor that foreign citizens would be permitted to visit their families in occupied countries.

I inquired at some office, was given a form, told to return it in person, duly filled out. I promptly did. Was told to inquire in one week's time. I did. Permission refused.

Distraught, almost in tears, I left the mean little window with the self-satisfied badge-wearing individual behind it. As I walked down the stone steps, a booted brute in the brown uniform thrust at me a tray of the trinkets sold weekly on the streets for the benefit of the party or some equally worthy cause.

"*Nein danke*," I said, pushing away the tray.

A stamping of boots, an outpouring of angry words greeted my gesture. It was a patriotic duty to buy those trinkets, didn't I know?

I saw passersby staring over their shoulders as they left the area as fast as they could.

I don't know why I did not get more upset than I did. I felt almost elated as I steadily walked away without buying any trinket. I did not even tell Abel about the incident for several months. I was acquiring a thicker skin, I guess.

I had not been used to that sort of treatment. As a French woman, I had always been treated well, even favored at times. If that brute had known I was French, he would probably not have screamed at me. The thought amused me.

The Nazis, I think, never knew how to classify the French. Poles, Russians, Jews were subhumans. Easy. But the French? Degenerate, immoral, eventually fated to turn into a half-breed race, yes, but . . . In spite of it all, somehow, the Nazis harbored a reluctant esteem for the French.

In early March, devastating air raids hit Berlin. A few days later, Abel received his new assignment: Yugoslavia. We were equally pleased, Abel because he loved the country, I because I thought he would be safe there. He departed. I waited for letters that soon arrived, enthusiastic as I had expected.

Abel was traveling on horseback, visiting mines the OT was exploiting. He would bring many sketches. Sketches, he wrote, that would be no more than images snatched at random by the lantern of a pilgrim straying in a nightly landscape. What was on both sides of the path would remain hidden to him. He did not mind, he loved the mystery as much as the beauty of Yugoslavia.

. . .

Four weeks later, Abel was back in Berlin, and I joined him.

He delivered to the OT the drawings he knew were expected, did not show the ones he had done for himself. There were many. I still have some.

One day, we learned from M. K., an employee at the OT's offices whom Abel had befriended, that there were well-organized partisan forces all over the Yugoslav territories. Didn't Abel know that?

"Glad I did not know," Abel said, laughing. "I wouldn't have ridden my horse so contentedly up and down the lovely hills and through the quaint villages asleep in the sun."

He had gone unarmed, as usual. He would have felt ridiculous carrying a gun, he said.

He remembered with glee an old woman who had served him food in an Orthodox village. She had refused to believe he was German.

"Serbski, Serbski," she kept repeating.

"Might help sometimes," he said, "to have some despicable Slavic features."

X X X V

We were in Berlin when Abel received his new assignment: Italy. Another country he loved.

In spite of all the lies the newspapers fed us, we knew that the German armies were rapidly losing ground in Russia and North Africa.

"Italy's next," Abel said. "But it will take time. The OT is going to have so much work to do there . . . I might still be needed."

Nearly every big city was getting bombed periodically now. We expected this to get worse. Nevertheless, I wanted to do some visiting before returning to Stuttgart. Overconfidence in my dumb luck, restlessness, dread of being alone in Stuttgart, I don't know what motivated me.

The day Abel took the train for Italy, I took the train for Leipzig. Abel's twenty-year-old niece, Hanne, was a student in a gymnastics school there. I decided to spend a few days with her and see Leipzig. The directress of Hanne's school was accommodating; she assigned me a room in the dormitory and permitted me to take the meager meals with the students in exchange for my rations.

Hanne was a strong, tall, outgoing girl with—a bit unusual in

Germany—dark eyes and hair. Every evening, we strolled together through the streets of the orderly, severe stone and cement city. I, the diminutive aunt, was duly impressed by the feeling of security the place communicated.

One evening, we passed the renowned Auerbachs Keller. Goethe, in his famous tragedy, *Faust,* had Mephistopheles accompany Dr. Faust to the Auerbachs Keller one night. Dr. Faust had just sold his soul in exchange for knowledge, power, and youth.

Hanne and I could not resist the urge, so we pushed open the door of the Auerbachs Keller. It had been left ajar. As it had been in Goethe's time, this was a place where men gathered to drink wine and beer and talk men's talk. We knew that.

A dignified, white-haired employee in uniform surged out of the duly darkened entrance hall to meet us. Hanne hurried to explain that her French aunt, who was visiting beautiful Leipzig for the first time, dearly wanted to see this world-famous landmark, the Auerbachs Keller.

The white-haired employee led us through the short, dark hall; we walked down two or three steps and found ourselves in a semidark room where elderly gentlemen sat at heavy wooden tables under a cloud of cigar and pipe smoke. We were formally introduced by the employee. The gentlemen smiled benignly. A small table, two small chairs, and two glasses of white wine were brought, courtesy of the patrons. Hanne and I modestly sat and sipped our wine.

Soon, conversations that our entrance had interrupted resumed, and we felt pleasantly left to ourselves.

I listened. I always listen. I often forget places, I rarely forget words.

Hamburg. I heard Hamburg, "the proud city by the sea." During a recent bombing even the streets had been burning. Now, now, a harbor not having water to extinguish the fire! The elderly gentlemen shook their heads, some pounded the table with their fists and laughed. . . .

And Nürnberg, well, Nürnberg, what do you expect? These little old houses, with their shingle roofs, they were no better than matchboxes. . . . More laughter.

Over 150 years had passed since Mephistopheles had played tricks on the naive drunks at the Auerbachs Keller. One hundred fifty years? *He* was still there in the spring of 1943, I swear. Only one more year and I would wonder how many of the foolish elderly gentlemen had survived the destruction of their city. Hanne survived. Her school did not.

From Leipzig I traveled to Nürnberg. A pleasant couple I had met a few months before in Sankt Anton had invited me to stay with them whenever I decided to visit their beautiful city. We had exchanged postcards. My visit was expected.

When the husband came to get me at the railroad station, the first thing I noticed was his party badge. He had not worn it in Austria. As a lawyer, I reflected, he probably had to be a party member. His suburban house was comfortable, his wife was a pretty blond, and their two lovely little daughters adored their handsome parents.

A peacetime dinner, vegetarian in my honor, was served by a maid. I don't think we talked about anything worth remembering. We had hardly retired when the sirens sounded. We spent part of the night in the cellar. The little daughters climbed into their father's lap. Their smiling mother served coffee and pastries. The bombing, not heavy, seemed to be reserved for the center of town.

To pass the time, the lawyer described to us how he imagined the future. In a couple of years, he said, we would be building whole cities underground. We had the technology, and we had the manpower. Oh, yes, yes, we would get used to it. We would live down there, perfectly safe and contented.

Next morning, I found the city renowned for its quaint medieval houses wrapped up in a shroud of gray gauze.

I walked on nearly deserted streets. Houses were smoldering away by themselves. A few trolleys ran. I stood transfixed in front of a gutted house: its tall stone walls were still standing; the high gable told how high and slanted the roof had been. There were workers around this particular house. One stood on top of an inner wall. He held up a long black beam by the middle. The blue-and-yellow burning end of the sinister giant match precariously hovered above a Virgin Mary of gray stone standing in its niche halfway to the lofty gable's top.

"Albrecht Dürer's house," a passerby stated in a toneless voice, and walked on.

It had taken only one instant in our murderous century to do away with a landmark that four centuries of turbulent history had respected.

The following day, I departed, expressing my thanks and my regrets about the destructive bombing. But my hosts were quick in reassuring me: nothing had been destroyed that could not be rebuilt, they said.

As the head of the family accompanied me to the railroad station, he confided that there was one thing he disliked about the National Socialist system, namely, the sheer impossibility of giving the correct "Heil Hitler" salute—right arm fully extended—on a rainy day when you had to carry a briefcase and an umbrella.

This was, I guessed, meant to be a joke.

XXXVI

❧

Back in Stuttgart, alone, I walked up the street to the French consulate, offered a wistful *bonjour* to a house dead behind its gray iron shutters and a sigh to the two hundred *pots de confiture* stored in the cellar. Still there, the sweet stuff peacefully shrinking in its glass jars, after three hungry years?

I had tea with the lady who had once asked me for French lessons. Her pale, finely chiseled face smaller than ever, she was preparing to move to her country house.

I don't know how this came about, but, in the course of the conversation, she revealed that my apartment had been previously occupied by her former teachers, two Jewish sisters whom she had liked very much. In 1939, they had been forced to move out, she said.

"Where did they go?" I asked.

"I don't know," she said. "I don't know."

At the publishing house, I inquired about the book translation that had been more or less promised to me a few months before. The project had fallen through, the editor said. But he gave me the address of someone in Berlin who needed translations into French. I wrote, got a prompt answer and an appointment for early July.

As soon as Abel returned to Berlin, about mid-June, I joined him. He had been allocated an apartment downtown within walking distance of Kurfürstendamm and of the beautiful, old-fashioned zoological garden.

The large apartment had been divided into two. The part we occupied comprised a large living room converted into an artist's studio—oversized table, bookshelves, easel—a small bedroom, bathroom, and kitchen. The kitchen had a curious feature: a bed installed on a platform tucked up between cupboards and ceiling; maid quarters, we were told. The ladder, necessary to gain access to these quarters, was no longer there.

There was only tepid water in the bathroom. It was summer, we did not need hot water. And there was not always gas for cooking. But then there was nothing to cook. We were delighted.

I could not tell today what we ate that summer. I remember the eggplants I spotted once from the trolley we were riding. We got off at the next stop, walked back, got two small eggplants. A long walk for a skimpy meal. And I remember the big bunches of watercress I once bought. Two days on a strict diet of watercress, and we had no doubt about its diuretic properties.

One evening, as we were climbing the stairs to our apartment, sirens wailed. The *Wächter* caught up with us and made us go down to the cellar. He wrote down our names, made sure he had every tenant in the cellar, and locked the door.

In the large, dusty, semidark cellar, there were, we guessed, over one hundred people, all assigned to their own particular areas. Old bathtubs filled with water were scattered around.

A young pregnant woman sat close to us. She shrieked whenever a bomb fell, then smiled in confusion.

I read a Balzac novel that night. I always carried a book with me in case we were forced into some cellar. My remedy against claustrophobia.

My dear, I was reading by the light of one weak bulb dangling from a beam, *My dear, their souls wear white gloves.* This was a gentleman telling a lady about . . . Englishmen.

I chuckled, wanted to tell Abel. A bomb, English no doubt, fell close by. The young woman let out a long shriek. Lights went out.

Later, much later, sirens sounded the all clear and the *Wächter* unlocked the door. We filed out, craving fresh air. There was no fresh air, only the stench of things burning. The sky was black with ashes. All the stars were dead. Abel and I had the same thought: I don't want to die down there with these people. Snobs. As if we had the choice. We shrugged, went to bed.

"If the house starts to burn, I'll jump out of the window, and you will follow me," Abel said the next day.

Our third-floor apartment opened onto a large square court, once a flower garden, now churned-up dark soil and weeds.

"It's soft ground," Abel said. "We can jump."

"And break one leg—or two."

"You have got to know how to jump. I'll teach you."

Back in the faraway happy days, Abel used to accompany friends to the climbing school of Fontainebleau. The friends would practice climbing the vertical faces of high rocks there. Abel would get to the top by taking the easy back path, then, legs folded up, he would jump and land on the soft, sandy soil below. No one I knew remembered anyone ever attempting the same feat. Abel was filmed once as he jumped, holding an open umbrella as a parachute.

I could not tell today how high the rocks were. Not as high as our third-floor apartment in Berlin, surely.

In order to teach me to jump, Abel took me to one of the several lakes close to the city. The one we went to, easy to reach by trolley, had black water. One big floating tree trunk, loosely secured at both ends, separated shallow from deep-water areas. A wooden scaffolding, gray with age, provided two diving boards, one three meters high, the other ten.

Most swimmers were lighthearted young soldiers who bore nasty red scars.

Neither their friendly encouragement nor Abel's urgings could persuade me to plunge into the gloomy waters from the high diving board.

We often went to the black lake. Bits of paper would float down sometimes from a sky still gray with ashes from the previous night's bombing. Complemented the color of the lake, Abel said.

We never again went down to our building's cellar. Never answered the *Wächter's* banging on our door. We stood at the window, watching the splendid, deadly game.

Parachute flares, mimicking glowing small moons of many colors, leisurely descended, painting on a night robbed of its stars a Christmas tree as big as the sky. Long daggers of white light stabbed at the heavens, catching planes in their luminous conic snares. Some planes escaped. Some did not but plunged straight down in brief, fiery death.

Detonations would throw us around a bit sometimes. Once, I remember, we had been standing at the bedroom window when a bomb fell close by. Propelled through an open door like a bundle of laundry, I found myself sprawling on the living room floor ten meters away. Abel stood on his head in the middle of the bed. We laughed. . . . We laughed. A sign of neither courage nor madness, just that peculiar drunken behavior that disaster induces sometimes.

Whenever the sky was not darkened by ashes or smoke, the days were beautiful. Absolutely beautiful. And oh, so calm.

Were there many beautiful days? I remember many.

Dizzy days, sleepwalking days.

"Don't even need to watch your step," Abel said. "Doesn't help."

XXXVII

The sun would not shine over Berlin on that summer morning of July 1943. The trolleys would not run either. I had an appointment at 10 A.M. with someone who needed translations into French.

"I'll walk," I had said. "Hope the streets aren't burning."

"And some worthy gentleman is not dead and buried, and his publishing company has not gone up in smoke . . . You have got to have a guardian angel!" Abel had said.

We had survived the night. We laughed.

I rarely went out alone, but that day I did.

At 9 A.M. there was a bright sun and a vast blue sky way up beyond the smoke and ashes that hovered over the city. The light that filtered through was like the light of dawn. Reassuring: no air raids on cloudy days. An acrid smell pervaded the air. Not too bad that day. The silence was disquieting. God knows, it should have been welcome after the atrocious racket of the night. The mutilated city was refusing to wake up.

The streets I walked were deserted, whether the houses on both sides had been demolished or left intact, deserted and singularly clean, as if the ruined buildings had swallowed up their own rubble.

A few feet away, right in front of me, a man, a woman, and a child shuffled out from under an archway onto the sidewalk. Bent, in clothes turned shabby overnight and soiled with bits of plaster, they did not bother to brush off. They trudged on, keeping close to the walls, the man leading the way. The first ones to dig themselves out, or the last ones, or the only ones. They turned a corner. Gone. As if they had never been there.

Not quite real. That was how everything was then. Just going to one of the rare good restaurants that still opened in the evening was unreal. There was always an unseemly cluster of people bigger than I massed against the dark glass revolving restaurant doors. But Abel placed me at the strategic point, and when the doors revolved, I was soon propelled inside. I would fast secure a table before rearranging hat and coat. Abel would come, and we would celebrate.

All we ever got was the illusion of a meal. But sometimes a French waiter would procure a bottle of wine or a double serving of some so-called dessert.

Once we shared a table with a portly gentleman in a black suit. "A banker," he said. "An artist," Abel said. The banker handed over his precious fountain pen and pencil set.

"You'll put this to better use than I ever could," he said glumly.

His cavernous ground-floor apartment, where we went for an after-supper drink, was cluttered with crates and cardboard boxes. We sat on crates to drink a potent crystal-clear liqueur.

"French women keep tiny vials of this handy," I said. "Hamamelis . . . old remedy against monthly discomfort."

The banker roared with laughter, could hardly stop.

We didn't have much to tell him, or he to tell us. So he wound up his phonograph and put on a recording. A tango. Abel's favorite.

"Dance," the banker said, shoving boxes to make room. "Dance."

Ages before, in Paris, Abel and I had danced, danced. . . . This night, in Berlin, we danced—in memoriam.

Alarm sirens wailed through the night. Next, we knew, the building warden would come pounding on doors, order everybody to the cellar, write down our names and keep us locked up, down there, until the alarm was over.

"*Nein, nein,*" the banker whispered and stopped the music.

We went on dancing. He handed us an open umbrella to hold over our heads. Then he climbed on a pile of crates and poured a carafe full of water over the umbrella. He was immensely entertained.

Alarm over, we walked home. Beautiful, clear night. Summer nights never got very dark over Berlin. Once more Abel told me, "Berliners are mad."

Maybe so.

Supper at M. K.'s place. (M. K. worked for the Organization Todt, gave Abel his assignments, which, at the moment, consisted of illustrating books put out for Organization Todt workers.) M. K.'s newly started collection of ancient ceramics was displayed all over his large apartment. Reminded me of Abel buying a grand piano when the first bombs began to fall. Men have to prove that they can spit into the Furies' faces.

"I am going to walk off with the Chinese blue cat," I said.

Supper: potatoes fried without fat. And wine. Jokes. Bitter, silly. We laughed a lot. Somebody said something we never say: "We may die tonight. Are you ready? I am."

Abel groaned. Cool, collected M. K. exploded: "What? Ready to die? Me? Never. I have got to be there when it all ends . . . standing on the rubble!"

Tall, so thin he couldn't hold his back straight, a baby's complexion, pale, curly hair. Standing on a pile of rubble?

"With that rage in his heart, he might make it though," Abel said.

And so would the pale, resolute, young woman we saw in the café on Kurfürstendamm. Did we know, she asked, that Goebbels had ordered all the young women with babies to be evacuated—to Poland, of all places?

"Not me," she suddenly shouted, and people turned around. "If a hundred stay, I'll be one of them. If twenty stay, I'll be one of them. If only one stays . . . I'll be that one!"

Ignorant young Berliner, paraphrasing Victor Hugo! I was ecstatic.

"*Die Schufte, Die Shufte,*" Abel said. "You're getting as mad as the rest of them!"

"Maybe so. I don't care."

At the zoo was a leopard that had a large enclosure to himself, a lawn, a tree, a gingerbread house, and a warden who entered the enclosure freely, speaking to the leopard as if he were a person.

We went to the zoo nearly every day. It was close to where we lived, and the entrance fee was modest. Quite a place, the zoo. Crowds of thin people placidly watching big cats feasting on giant roasts and steaks and monkeys fastidiously peeling bananas and sucking on oranges. The only place where such food could be seen. The government, somebody whispered to us, did not dare to evacuate the zoo!

One day the leopard and I walked toward each other. The icy convex mirrors of his golden eyes were riveted on me. We met at the enclosure. He rubbed his head against it. I pushed my fingers through the chain link, scratched him behind the ear. He purred a startling loud purr, and, eyes shut, licked my fingers with an extravagantly rough tongue.

Abel, pale, grabbed my arm.

"It will bite off a finger or two someday," a well-dressed old gentleman commented.

I answered with a triumphant smile.

Abel finally pulled me away. The old gentleman was still standing on the same spot, leaning on his cane, his colorless eyes fixed on some image way beyond us.

"What can he be seeing?"

"Elephants, crocodiles, serpents cut to pieces, SS shooting a leopard in an apartment across the street. . . ." Abel said.

A furious rumbling startled me. Twenty feet away, a flatbed truck crossed the street with a load of tall, slim policemen in ankle-length gray-green coats, black boots, and headgear well shined. They stood or lay stretched out, perfect, alike, rigid, in life or death, tin soldiers out of a drugged dream. Then they too were gone.

The slice of sky I could see between jagged rooftops was still slate gray. Bits of paper detached themselves from the grayness and floated down, mimicking dirty snowflakes. I walked on, watching them, the only things that moved. They grew larger suddenly. Book pages! They were book pages! Hundreds of them, waving and fluttering before meeting the pavement with a last shiver. The publishing house could not be—or have been—too far away. I chuckled nervously.

And there it was, a slim six-story building advancing like the prow of a boat where two streets met at a narrow angle, *Deutsche Verlag* spelled in smudged white at the top of a black door. The door did not hang right, and windowpanes were shattered, but the building was standing. Standing. I ran to the door, came to a stop, and ran back across the street. Coming out of the building was a buzzing I did not trust. Unexploded bombs often went off during the day, emitting, I imagined, that kind of sound before exploding. I waited across the street, began to feel foolish, ventured back.

The buzzing was still on. A machine? Machines? Printing machines? The heavy entrance door, ajar and hanging askew, was stuck, but I could squeeze in. The elevator did not run. I had not expected it to. There were stairs. I started to climb them, reached the second landing. Partition walls had been blown out. I peered into vast semidark rooms. Lightbulbs dangling here and there gave some light. Men stood beside machines. Machines hummed.

The third landing was blocked by a printing press. I climbed over it, went on. The fourth and fifth floors, as far as I could see, were intact. The sixth floor had been recently built or rebuilt. The rough, unpainted lumber of the floors and doors had not lost its scent of too green wood. "Sixth floor, number 7," my appointment letter said. I knocked on door number 7 at 10:15.

"*Herein!*" a strong masculine voice answered.

I went in. A short, middle-aged, ruddy-faced man in a uniform the color of goose shit—as it gladdened our hearts to say—jerked from behind a small, brand-new desk, his right arm extended.

"*Heil* Hitler!" he shouted.

People baked and crushed every night in their own cellars, survivors digging themselves out, scrounging for food to sustain another day of life. "*Heil* Hitler." Armies cut to pieces. "*Heil* Hitler."

"*Grüss Gott,*" I said.

The man paid no attention, he rushed from behind his desk, grabbed a hand I had not extended, and shook it, smiling eagerly. Perspiring too, I noticed. He handed me a thin book—a mystery—pointing proudly at the author's name—his. How long would it take me to translate it? he wanted to know.

I opened the book at random. Poor stuff, I decided.

"Three months, about."

"There will be more," the man said, and he indicated other slim books lined up on a single shelf.

"These books are being published for the benefit of the French volunteer workers," he explained. "They will have to be adapted for the French taste, you understand."

Yes, I understood, and yes, I could do that too. I looked down at the gorgeous Aryans depicted on the garish book cover; count on me, I would fix them.

The man quoted a fee. Fair, probably. I did not care, there was nothing to buy.

"It's snowing book pages all around, did you notice?" I could not help myself, I had to say it.

But nothing could dampen the pride and elation of an author whose books were about to be translated into French.

"That's nothing. We shall print more and more books!"

Less than two years later, when the French troops would announce themselves by shooting at the house where I lived, there would be on my table a German mystery—the fourth—waiting to be adapted for the French taste.

That day when I came home, Abel was working on a book illustration, a battle between the Goths and the Romans in 500 A.D. or so.

"One Goth, one Roman." He was counting the dead.

"The Goths won, I think," I said.

"One Goth, one Roman," Abel said.

XXXVIII

❦

On August 3, 1943, Hamburg suffered severe bombings that triggered firestorms. *"Die Katastrophe"* could not be minimized. People asphyxiated by the thousands, burned to death as they tried to run across asphalt streets on fire. Forty thousand killed in one night. We knew it all the next day.

We left Berlin shortly after, scheduled to return three weeks later.

In Stuttgart, the complacency of earlier days had been shaken. Many were quietly leaving town. Abel's mother was easily persuaded to depart with her grandson. She would stay with one of her daughters, who resided in a small town in the Black Forest. Abel's older brother had moved to the countryside with wife and daughters.

We had dinner one evening at the house of our acquaintance, the lawyer. Pessimistic and angry as ever, he declared briefly that he was needed in town and would stay.

I hardly knew his wife, yet we felt like sisters; she too was from one of the conquered countries.

At some point, before we sat at the table, I mentioned that one early morning in December 1941, I had, from the window at the Kunstgewerbeschule, watched many people climbing into buses. I had been wondering ever since who these people had been.

"They were the Jews of Stuttgart," the lawyer said. "And they were put on a train that never arrived anywhere.

"They were put on a train that never arrived anywhere," he repeated. "Do you understand what I am saying?"

No, I did not understand.

He turned his back on me and got into an animated talk with Abel. Soon they were describing the refined tortures they would inflict upon the infamous clique at the helm, the day they would lay their hands on them. Dead serious and enraged, they went on topping each other in cruelty.

The lawyer's wife and I got sick listening to them. We took refuge in the kitchen and slammed the door shut.

"Are all men insane?" the young wife asked, her small face narrower and her big eyes filling with tears.

I don't remember what I answered.

It was shortly afterward that Abel told me he would have tried to kill Hitler if he had not had me.

"I would probably not have succeeded," he added. "I am not clever enough, but I would have tried, at least tried."

"Would you prefer Himmler, or Goering?" I asked.

"Either tried . . . or died of shame."

Then Abel decided that he was not going to let me stay alone in Stuttgart.

"We are going to find a place in the country," he said.

Over the years, he had kept contact with a family of farmers for whom he had worked as a teenager during the First World War. We had spent a few Sundays at their farm after this new war had started. They had never let us go home without presents, usually an enormous loaf of homemade bread and a few pounds of wheat berries. This was precious food for us.

The farmer owned good land, cattle and horses, and a big three-story house in which a small apartment was reserved for the next daughter to marry.

We would be able, we thought, to rent this empty apartment for one year or so. The sixty-year-old farmer had remarried late in life and had several daughters still too young to get married. We knew him as a rather dour Lutheran. He ate his Sunday meals with his guests in a vast, bare living room while wife and daughters ate theirs in the cavernous dark kitchen. On Sunday afternoons, he read the Bible. By himself. Nevertheless, we were full of hope the Sunday morning we took the train for Herrenberg, a town some fifty kilometers south of Stuttgart.

We walked for one hour or so through well-tended fields of wheat, corn, beets, potatoes, and poppies (poppy seeds make good oil). The harvest was in season, but no one worked on Sunday, and the fields were deserted. We reached the small village, a nearly treeless cluster of tall gray farmhouses loosely grouped around the church, a solid building that had neither a steeple nor an ornamented portal.

As usual, we were warmly greeted by the whole family. But when Abel mentioned our desire to rent the apartment, the farmer turned cold and severe.

"This apartment is reserved for my daughter when she gets married. Can't be rented," he said firmly.

We understood, the matter could not be discussed.

"You should have more confidence in our *Führer*," he said. "He will take care of things in his own time. Always has. Cities are suffering. Yes, indeed! God always punishes the sinners. Sodom and Gomorrah . . . remember?"

The women might have wanted to have me around: I could sew, and they did not have time for sewing. Besides attending to their multiple female duties in the household, they worked in the fields like the men. But they were not consulted.

The army officer brother-in-law came to the rescue. He had been transferred to Stuttgart. We often saw him. He remembered having seen a picturesque old house once when wandering through the Black Forest.

"The farmers told me it was haunted," he said. "Might still be empty!"

He inquired and soon found the landlord's address. We wrote. Got a prompt answer. The house had just been rented, sight unseen, to a lady who lived in Stuttgart. But in case she changed her mind after seeing it, the owner wrote, we would be the first on his list, we had such fine recommendations.

Less than a week later, at noontime, a few bombs fell on downtown Stuttgart. The renter of the haunted house was killed in her bathtub, and the house was ours.

I remember feeling uneasy about this peculiar stroke of luck. But in dangerous times, scruples of that sort have a short life.

XXXIX

Early one morning, we boarded a train that was to take us 130 kilometers farther south. Closer and closer to Switzerland, we said, and felt childishly happy about that.

Hours later, we got out at a tiny railroad station built on a hill above Bergheim, our goal, a village where the houses, hugging each other, stood around a church perched on its own low hill.

We walked down unpaved but neat Main Street, greeted by the nurturing smells of plowed earth and farm animals. The two-story houses along the street, whitewashed, topped by high gray shingle roofs, were unassuming and somehow friendly.

On another low hill, a building with large windows and a slanted red tile roof had a Nazi flag hanging limply by the door. City Hall, surely.

We walked up to it. The door opened before we knocked.

We said: "Grüss Gott!"

The farmer-secretary said: "Grüss Gott!"

We handed him our rent contract, he registered us as new residents of the village of Bergheim, gave us one big key, and volunteered directions.

"Follow the road to the end," he pointed at Main Street, "three kilometers or so. . . . At the end of the road there is a farm. Just before the farm, you will see a weg [path] on your right. That's where you go down into the *Schlucht* [ravine], down, down, until you see a house by the brook. Can't miss it . . ." He chuckled. "And so, you think you want to live down there. . . ." He waved us on our way, shaking his head.

We followed Main Street past a church that had a steeple and a portal. A village church so like the one in the French village where I had been raised that, after half a century, their two images have melted into one another in my memory. I could not today describe either one with any certainty.

Out of the village we found ourselves on a plateau. On both sides of the narrow gravel road, a quilt of small rectangular fields. I recognized the pale stubble of barley and rye. Potato and clover fields made patches of green. Far apart, on the plateau that stretched to the horizon, a few low houses with high roofs under clumps of trees.

The road went straight and even for a while, then meandered gently downhill.

We passed a little house tucked into a fold of lush green turf, its shingle roof and red-brick chimney at the level of the road, willows and ash trees waving golden leaves over it. Close by, in a meadow, a big white horse quiet as a statue, and beyond it all, the dark edge of a forest. Who could be living in this fairy-tale house? I asked myself.

Half a kilometer or so farther, the road ended in the yard of the only farm there. On the right was the path we were to take. It went down between a rocky cliff to which bushes and small crooked trees clung and a steep slope overgrown with tall trees. Rarely used, uneven, slippery, dark, it was barely wide enough for a farmer's cart.

We walked down.

After ten minutes or so, we heard water gurgling. The path got steeper, turned slightly, and there, in a clearing below, was the haunted house. Massive, white under a high gray shingle roof, the second floor advancing over the first, medieval style: the perfect picture of the secluded abode in a classical frame of rocks, trees, and mountain stream.

The haunted house

This was a five-hundred-year-old grist mill that the mountain stream, in a fit of spring madness, had destroyed some thirty years before, Abel's brother-in-law had told us. Rebuilt as living quarters, it had been, in turn, a café—odd location for a café—and the refuge of a poet. For the past fifteen years or so, the only tenants, reputedly, had been ghosts. Until we, who feared bombs more than ghosts, had come along.

We approached gingerly, more amazed and intrigued than we wanted to admit, stumbling over the ancient stone grinding wheel, bone-white, edged with green grass, embedded in the ground, tombstone and doormat.

We opened the heavy entrance door that gave out a classic groan. There was a small dark entrance hall and, on the right, two steps down, a vast square room, its windows at ground level, a dozen old chairs standing against the back wall. The café's chairs? We could use some, I said.

On the left, a few steps down, a cool shallow cellar, one wall and floor rough bare rock.

One short, steep flight of stairs up a wide, semidark hall led to a long, narrow balcony. At one end, rustic, well built, the toilet. Five rooms opened into the hall: one medium and two large ones, one small kitchen, and a pleasant living room that had a big, square, bright-green ceramic stove.

Another steep flight of stairs up and we were in an attic, large enough for additional comfortable living quarters. One room had been built. A lovely room: dark wood paneling covered its walls and ceiling; a stove of ornate, pale-green ceramic reached nearly up to the ceiling, beautiful and comforting. A small stained-glass window opening onto the roof represented a bearded man in profile: the poet, surely.

The front window opened onto a landscape squeezed between, on the right, a sixty-meter-high vertical cliff of yellow and orange rock and, on the left, beyond the brook, a steep slope overgrown with evergreen and deciduous trees. The shallow brook ran under a rustic narrow bridge, then, gurgling, glittering over polished stones, vanished under the trees at the bottom of the ravine. Could this quaint stream have given centuries of life to a grist mill and then destroyed it?

"There will still be plenty of room for a ghost or two after we move in," Abel said.

By the time we left in the afternoon, we could tell the hours of sunlight would be short at the bottom of the *Schlucht*. Never mind, we had found a safe place.

X L

e returned to Stuttgart and started to pack.

The use of a truck to transport furniture was *verboten*. Every item, packed or unpacked, had to be sent piecemeal by train. Crates or boxes were not available, paper and string scarce.

We congratulated each other for having acquired so little. We abandoned a cumbersome kitchen cabinet, I vaguely remember.

Transporting pianos was *verboten.*

"Oh, never mind," Abel said. "It was stupid to buy a piano anyway."

"Write a sentimental letter to a piano mover," I suggested.

Nonsense. Abel only shrugged.

I nagged until he wrote.

No answer came. None was expected.

ur good-byes were few. Abel's mother, older brother, and family had left town, younger brother was enlisted, Christine's husband was out of town.

We stopped at the office of our friend the lawyer.

"Come for dinner tonight," he said. "Might have some surprise for you."

Indeed, there was another guest we knew: "One of Hitler's first sixty companions." Abel had slapped his face, and he had promised we would be *vernichted*. Two years before. Only two years?

The Nazi greeted us as if we had been dear old friends.

We smiled, said little.

We had drinks, talked about trifles.

After the meal, Abel and I danced to French music. Easier than to talk. The Nazi watched as if highly interested.

"I know a nightclub owner in Berlin," he suddenly exclaimed. "I am going to see to it, personally . . ."

Abel and I sat down, laughing.

But the man was dead serious.

"I will find a niche for you," he insisted. "I will."

Had he gone mad too?

"No," our lawyer friend said later on. "The old devil knows he has lost the game. Has to make believe he is still in charge of something . . ."

XLI

❧

We finally departed in October, taking with us a few large paintings, happy days' memories too precious to be shipped without crating. Since we expected to have to camp for some time, we also carried with us the old sleeping bags that surely would bring back dreams of Mediterranean shores.

Our heavy winter coats we left hanging in a closet. Abel would pick them up when he came back to check the mailbox. Mail, for unknown reasons, could not be forwarded.

To our surprise, by the time we arrived, our belongings, every one of them, had already gathered at Bergheim's railroad station, overwhelming the old employee.

By afternoon, our next-door neighbor—the farmer who lived on top of the cliff—had loaded our things onto a cart. A few hours later, at the ravine's entrance, he added one ox to his team of one horse and a helper to lead the animals.

He walked beside the cart. I followed at some distance, imagining a variety of possible mishaps.

One place on the steep trail, I had observed, was badly washed out. Sure enough, when the cart came to it, it tilted precariously over the edge. But the farmer was ready; with arms outstretched, he steadied the load while his helper hurried the animals. The perilous descent proceeded.

The two men easily carried our light furniture up the stairs. We slept in our own bed that night. In the poet's room.

A few days later, Abel started back to Stuttgart. A new OT assignment would surely be in the mailbox. He did not mind sleeping on the floor in the empty apartment. The winter coats, he said, would make good blankets.

As I walked with him to the railroad station, I suggested that he spend the night at his older brother's new lodgings in a small town only three or four train stations before Stuttgart. For some reason, Abel did not want to.

We argued for a while.

"Your brother surely will have one good bottle of wine in the cellar," I said.

As he boarded the train, Abel promised he would stay at his brother's house overnight. That night, Stuttgart was bombed and our former neighborhood was hard hit.

Abel walked up the hill, and from the street he was able to see his piano. Our apartment's back wall, roof, and windows had been blown out. The lower floors and stairs were intact, and the people who had been in the cellar were unhurt. But a neighbor who had remained in her third-floor apartment had been killed.

The piano was covered with chunks of plaster but otherwise undamaged. Our winter coats, still hanging in the closet, were only dusty. In the mailbox, Abel found the new OT assignment for Botzen (northern Italy).

"A shame," he said. "I wanted to go to Naples."

The American army had entered Naples a few days before.

. . .

On a fine late-October day, Abel left for Berlin. He had to get instructions and an itinerary before leaving for Italy. His first letter depicted the latest calamities. Exactly three weeks after we had left, downtown Berlin had been badly bombed. The house to which we had been scheduled to return had burned to the ground. One hundred twenty people had baked in the cellar. Three had managed to dig themselves out. There had been a massacre at the zoo—seven elephants torn to pieces, serpents and crocodiles crawling on the streets, destroyed, big cats hiding in neighboring houses until shot by the SS. The morning after the bombing, our favored female orangutan had fallen from a tree, dead of a heart attack, when her keeper had called her. All that while we had been discovering the perfect shelter and feeling quite smug about it.

I did not have much time to reflect about this new stroke of uncanny good luck. New tenants for the haunted house suddenly showed up: a woman and her grown-up daughter—plus their enormous cartloads of furniture, duly crated.

Well, I told myself, this house can accommodate two families, and it will probably be more pleasant not to be alone during the winter months. Less than a week later, Frau Döhnker, my cotenant, proudly informed me that her husband was a high-ranking army officer—almost a general—and her two sons SS men. Then I knew that solitude would have been preferable.

Frau Döhnker decreed that we would share living room and kitchen.

I did not say but decided I would share nothing.

Since we were all classified as refugees, a kitchen stove, a small round wood-burning stove, and one cord of wood had automatically been allocated to each family.

I made a kitchen and dining room out of one of the large first-floor rooms, where a rickety round table already stood, and a spare bedroom out of the smallest back room. The poet's room was going to be my bedroom, living room, and work room.

Pleased to have three times as much space as I had, Frau Döhnker generously insisted the living room be a common room—provided I helped with the heating, of course.

I discovered, in the back of the old mill, a stable large enough for one or two goats. I remembered the goat we had brought home one evening, my father and I. I was ten then, and my baby sister had needed wholesome goat milk. When my neighbor's bright-eyed fourteen-year-old daughter, Emma, brought me a beautiful orange kitten, I thanked her and, in the same breath, told her that I needed a goat.

Emma's parents were simple people who led a hard, lonely life working their rather miserly land. They had welcomed an opportunity to make a bit of money when Abel and I had asked for their help. And they had been gracious about it, inviting us for a snack and a talk. They welcomed outsiders who could perhaps explain to them things they could not understand, mainly this terrible war that so bewildered them.

With the help of Emma's parents, I bought a goat from one of their relatives, then a sheep, and, to feed them over the winter, a cartload of hay that filled up half of the vast attic.

Abel wrote often, melancholy yet optimistic letters. He was in the mountains of northern Italy—beautiful mountains—bicycling, sketching, regretting only that I was not with him, hoping to come for Christmas.

Irmgard, a slim girl of sixteen, did the mailman's job. She walked six kilometers to bring me one letter, and always smiled. She was the daughter of a farmer who was also the party boss.

In November, a notice from the railroad came indicating that a grand piano addressed to my husband had arrived at Bergheim railroad station. Remove promptly. No bill. Unknown sender.

On a snowy evening, a farmer from the village who owned a self-made flat contraption, mounted on tractor wheels and drawn by a horse, transported the piano. It was covered with potato sacks, and for part of the way, a bundled-up woman and her two children sat on it. I walked by its side on the narrow road.

At the ravine's entrance, our neighbor, with cart, horse, ox, and three of the strongest, youngest middle-aged men around, took over. Abel's piano came down a path made slippery by fresh snow, then, with some difficulty and one sprained back, was hauled up the stairs and installed in my spare bedroom. To comfort it, I lighted a fire in the small round wood-burning stove. Often that winter, I would sit on the piano bench, the orange cat curled up in my lap, and strike a few lonely notes that invariably broke my heart. As invariably, the friendly clawing of my cat would remind me of the riches I still possessed.

Abel's sister, the army officer's wife, lived in a town about thirty kilometers away. Herself a fine musician, she soon located a piano tuner, a silent, sickly-looking, middle-aged man. It took him over a week to do the job. He liked goat milk, he said, the modest vegetarian meals I concocted, and the blessed silence of the *Schlucht*.

I now belonged to the privileged class that would not get fat but would not starve. I had enough potatoes and apples to last me through the winter, a barrel of sauerkraut in the cellar, milk, and bread.

Three or four kilometers down the ravine, at the confluence of our small stream with a larger one, was a fine grist mill where I could buy flour. The miller's wife and I shared the same political hatreds, and this had made us instant friends. I always got much more than my skimpy rations of flour and grits.

I could bake my own good bread. Yeast being taboo to German vegetarians, I had learned to bake with whey. A blessing, since precious yeast could be bartered only for bacon or butter. And thus I settled down, playing at being a primitive little farmer. Enjoying the hardship as if it were the price to be paid for safety, I added to it, wading barefoot in the snow to take my daily morning dip in our icy mountain stream. I also, probably, wanted to show my Nazi cotenants how tough a little French woman could be.

When I finally sat down to do the translation I was supposed to deliver in three months' time, one month had already passed. I proceeded directly in longhand. No correcting, no rewriting. Saving time. And paper. I did adaptation for the French taste, as required, turning tall, blond, handsome Aryans into short, darker non-Aryans. Some types even got wavy hair and fleshy noses.

I wrote to Abel that our safe heaven had been invaded by the enemy and that I was not too happy about it.

He blissfully answered: "Might be interesting to observe the beast at close range. Too bad it has by now lost so much of its virulence."

XLII

꧁✦꧂

The almost-general husband, the SS sons, and, finally, Abel came down the snowy trail for Christmas. The verdigris uniform of the army and the velvety, strong green uniform of the SS soldiery paraded for one another's benefit. Black boots trampled virgin snow. And all the while, Abel filled the haunted house with the accents of Berlioz (French), Chopin (Polish), and Mendelssohn (Jewish). A special program for the barbarians.

They invited us for the *Bescherung* on Christmas eve: the distribution of Christmas presents. Abel and I sat in the living room, close to each other. And close to the door, I remember. No Christmas tree. Three soldiers in full regalia and three women—a sister-in-law, small, blond, possibly mute, had shown up—offered one another loot from the conquered countries: blond leather gloves from France I could never forget, and perfumes, coffee, tea, chocolate.

We were offered nothing, not even a cup of tea.

We soon took our leave.

"They don't know what time it is," Abel said.

He went to his piano, played a funeral march, adding variations.

The following day, we were invited to Frau Keller's, one of our neighbors' distant relatives, an elderly widow who ran her out-of-the-way small farm—three cows and a few fields—single-handed, or nearly so. Help would come when needed. For, in this scattered community of women and old or sick men, there was a tacit custom: whoever needed help got it somehow. No money involved.

Frau Keller had needed songs sung around a scrawny evergreen snatched in the *Schlucht* under the cover of night: her Christmas tree. It was *verboten* to cut tree or flower there: *Natur Schutz Gebiet* (natural protected area).

It had been Emma's unspoken duty to find singers. She had rounded up a few children, Abel, a musician, and me.

Abel's mother and one of his sisters—they now lived less than one hour away by train—joined our meager chorus to great advantage. Abel's mother, a natural singer, at seventy-five still had a fine soprano voice; his sister sang second part quite well.

Frau Keller, tall and massive in her ample black Sunday clothes, her broad, ruddy face set in an ecstatic smile, conjured up mounds of rich cookies and great bowls of heavenly whipped cream.

Christmas 1943, the fifth of an endless war.

Strolling through the village one day, we met Pfarrer Schnur, the tall, lean Catholic priest. In no time at all, we discovered that he shared our sorrows, angers, and hopes. And he was well informed. He knew more than Abel did about the battles at sea. He knew that in Italy, the American army had reached Cassino, 140 kilometers south of Rome.

"There are so many of us," I told Abel.

"No, there are not," Abel said. "We just attract each other and lose perspective."

. . .

A t the haunted house, we all did our best to avoid each other. But one day, at noontime, the almost-general, his wife, Abel, and I found ourselves standing together in front of the house. Attracted, probably, by the bit of sun that reached the ravine's bottom at noon. Thirty minutes of it at this time of year.

We exchanged a few remarks, stiffly.

I was thinking about what Frau Döhnker, a talkative person frustrated in our surroundings, had once told me: her husband had wanted to be in the SS, but they had not wanted him. Tall and slim, he wore the uniform well. Not enough of a qualification?

I always avoided looking at Frau Döhnker. She had a prominent goiter I did not care to see.

Suddenly I heard her raised voice.

"It is my belief," she was saying, "it is my belief that at the moment, it is the duty of every German to wear the soldier's uniform and carry a gun!"

There was an uneasy silence. I saw a throbbing under the yellow-gray skin of the goiter as Frau Döhnker looked up at her husband, seeking approval. But the husband looked away.

Abel, standing there in his old ski pants, favorite white sweater, and wooden clogs, suddenly spoke.

"Carry a gun? Me? Me? Listen . . . if I ever carry a gun . . ." He paused. "If I ever carry a gun . . . it will be . . . to shoot the likes of you!"

He had not stumbled over the last words.

I cringed.

Frau Döhnker chose to laugh.

"Oh, Oh, Herr, Herr Mrock . . ." She garbled the name. "*Bitte, bitte,* you don't mean that, no, you don't, we know you don't."

The almost-general was striding toward the house. He took off his military cap and stooped slightly as he passed the old door, which was too low for him. Small skull for such a tall man, I noted.

Frau Döhnker followed her husband into the house.

Twilight descended into the *Schlucht*, the thirty minutes of sun were over.

"They will take revenge," I told Abel.

"No time left for that," he said.

XLIII

❧

January 1944. Early one morning, three soldiers in full regalia climbed up the muddy trail as they left the undignified shelter of a haunted house for the glories of the front.

One week or so later, Abel's less colorful departure took place.

Silence paired with the clammy gloom of winter to invade the old house. If despondency, self-pity, or some version of my mother's unforgotten neurasthenia did not follow in their wake, it was because of a cat, a sheep, and a goat.

The orange cat followed me into the woods like a stubborn ray of sun. She trotted behind me the whole three kilometers of twisting path along the brook's edge whenever I went to the grist mill to get flour. At the shallows, when I started jumping from rock to rock to cross the fifteen meters or so of unruly water, she screamed in panic. Foxes, giant owls, and wild boars inhabited the woods; I had to carry the cat over.

With a rucksack full of flour on my back and a frightened cat clutching at my neck, the return was hazardous.

My cat never learned to go across the brook at the shallows. But she learned to meow under the window of the poet's room whenever she wanted to come in. She learned to get into the basket tied to a rope that I lowered for her, and to stay put when I pulled up the rope and the basket ascended dizzily along the front of the house. She learned the reverse procedure whenever she wanted to go out.

She drank one cup of warm goat milk every day, but she alone provided for her supper's main course. She got more protein than I did. Every morning, I found, lined up on the granite threshold, four or five cleanly extracted mouse livers with gall bladders attached.

My young, snow-white sheep, orphaned at birth, had been raised by a young girl. He had acquired unusual habits. Whenever we met, I would bend over, and the sheep would put his two hard little hooves on my shoulders, bury his muzzle in the crook of my neck, and utter endearing sounds. When spring came, the animals roamed around, and soon the sheep had become so big and heavy that he would knock me flat on my back at every greeting. I took to running away or hiding behind a tree whenever I caught sight of him, which created much distress until he outgrew his foolish love for humankind.

The brown goat demanded care and respect before love. I carried down from the attic big baskets of hay, fetched fresh water from the river, and milked her twice a day. And on time too if I did not want to be greeted by loud knocking on the stable walls, vehement bleating, or my proffered water spilled over my feet.

When the winter nights turned cold, I dressed the goat in one of my warmest sweaters. Sometimes I even carried down from the kitchen a bucket filled with hot coals and sat with goat and sheep for a few hours.

But every day, my exigent goat gave me three liters of milk I could drink. Cow milk didn't agree with me. And I made cheese.

What remained of the long days, I spent maintaining fire at times in three different stoves, writing to Abel and rereading his letters, or putting down a medley of thoughts and observations on every scrap of paper I could find. And, of course, working on my overdue, dismal translations.

Emma, the only visitor to the haunted house, would sometimes fetch me for a simple meal with her family. During the winter months, the farmers had time to read the newspaper we were all obligated by law to subscribe to, discuss the news, and worry. They worried about things I did not expect them to worry or even know about.

"Tell me," Emma's father once said, "tell me, what is it that the Nazis have against the Jews?"

"I don't know," I said.

"You don't know?"

Emma's father was deeply disappointed that I, who had traveled, lived in Paris and Berlin, did not know more than he about something that had bothered him for a long time, he said. So he told me what he knew about the Jews.

"The Jews I have known sold me cows," he said. "In the old days, the cow handlers were Jews. Well . . . they never stole my money. They never sold me a sick cow or a blind ox! I have nothing against the Jews!"

One day, on my way to Bergheim, I stopped to talk to the man who lived in the fairy-tale house. He was tending to his big white horse in the meadow nearby. Tall, in his fifties, with a ruddy, well-nourished face, reddish hair and mustache, and small, inquisitive eyes, he reminded me of a red fox. He was the forest ranger, he said. At once he invited me in to meet his wife.

She was bent, rather desiccated-looking, but neatly dressed and friendly. She fitted well in the small family room with its wood-paneled walls, big ceramic stove, polished chest and table of dark wood.

"Ah, you live down there in the *Schlucht*, I am the oldest sister of Emma's father," she said and got busy placing on the table a big jar of honey, small glasses, teaspoons, and a tall, slender bottle of "Schwartz

Wald cherry Schnapps," so the forest ranger announced. The stuff was as clear as water.

We sat down, and I was taught how to pour honey into a small glass, then Schnapps, stir. and drink. *Sehr gut!*

I wondered for some time about the forest ranger's friendliness. I told Emma's parents about it. They did not say a word. As if they had not heard me.

A short time later, on my way to gather dry twigs from a sunny slope free of snow, I met the forest ranger. He was carrying his gun and grinning.

"Just got good news," he said. "The government is going to pay me one thousand marks every time I catch one escapee, dead or alive!

"There are not many these days. There used to be so many of them . . . on their way to Switzerland. That was when I was not paid to catch them. . . ."

XLIV

❧

There was only one mailbox in Bergheim, affixed to an outside wall of the railroad station. The old part-time employee would show up an hour before one of the two daily trains was due, stamp the few letters posted that day, and put them into a sealed box on the train. Nobody was sitting in a post office, busy "checking" outgoing mail, in Bergheim. Something to be grateful for.

The only grocery store in the village was located halfway up the hill to the railroad station. Tiny wooden floor always swept clean, counter polished, brass scales and all the brass knobs of some twenty grocery drawers shined, it was empty of edibles twenty-eight days out of thirty. Once a month, there would be some gray noodles—about one handful for every villager—and, perhaps, a bit of sugar.

I would sometimes stop by, on my way to the mailbox, just to exchange a few words with the store owner. A dignified, melancholy woman in tidy dark clothes and black apron, every strand of her graying hair always in place, she was in attendance in her empty store every day of the year. And also forever waiting for her husband to come on furlough. Too old to be a soldier, he had been enlisted as a mason and sent, eighteen months before, to faraway Poland. His letters were rare and said nothing.

"What is it that they are building in Poland? And my man never getting a furlough . . . Why?" this patient, polite woman would ask with barely controlled anger.

No one could give her an answer.

I am, like my beloved father and grandfather, an agnostic. But on Sundays, when the weather was good, I went to mass. This was my way of showing my allegiance to the political convictions I shared with Pfarrer Schnur. I might also have needed to hear the priest's voice, magnified under the high church roof, promise us all that one day, the good would triumph over the bad. And I may also have needed to hear the villagers sing hymns and to exchange greetings with them. They were reserved but not unfriendly.

One Sunday, I spoke with a farmer less reserved than the others. A tall, slightly bent man in his sixties. He wanted to know how I was getting along "down there" with my animals. He was thrilled, I could tell, by my modest attempts at "farming."

He introduced himself as Herr Dashlet.

"Sounds a bit French," I remarked.

Herr Dashlet smiled.

"My great-great . . . grandfather, five, six generations back, was a French soldier in Napoleon's army," he said. "Well, this faraway grandfather got tired of soldiering, I guess . . . decided to stay in Bergheim. . . ."

Herr Dashlet and I observed that our world was a small one. And we were pleased about it.

I became a friend of the Dashlet family. When in the village, I often pushed open the heavy front door of their house. It was never locked during the day. I entered a long, dark entrance hall and paused to listen to horse and cows moving on the other side of a partition wall. Inside the village, the stables, kept fastidiously clean, were part of the houses.

Every time I stepped into the hall of the Dashlets' house, it was as if the closeness of the animals, the quiet noises they made, their warmth, and their smells restored my confidence in life.

The living quarters were up one steep flight of stairs. Frau Dashlet, a small woman in dark clothes, or her daughter-in-law, a powerful blond, would always answer my knock on the door of the family room. They would make me sit at a table by the enormous cubic green ceramic stove. Then the daughter-in-law would go back to cleaning whatever she had been cleaning before I came in, and Frau Dashlet would take care of me. She would place on the table in front of me a large round loaf of bread, a pitcher of cider, a glass, a small wooden board with a large chunk of smoked bacon on it, and a knife, its blade sharpened to a sliver by generations of bacon eaters.

It was the day a chunk of smoked Schwartz Wald bacon was offered to me that I forgot I was a vegetarian.

Frau Dashlet would sit at some distance while I ate. Only when I was finished cutting my bacon in thin slices, munching on it with good bread, and washing it down with great gulps of cider, would she ask whether I had heard from my husband. Then she would want to know how I was getting along "down there" in the *Schlucht*. I would ask about her enlisted youngest son. And then we would talk about the war. She seemed to be so well informed that I was amazed. I knew only what I could guess from reading the grossly biased newspaper. Abel's letters said as little about the war as my father's rare letters, and for the same reasons.

Sometimes I did not quite know what to think. Once, I remember, the Germans captured hundreds of Americans at Anzio, a beachhead south of Rome. Frau Döhnker and her daughters went into ecstasies over this great victory. "Oh, we always knew Germany would win in the end," they told me.

I could not wait to ask Frau Dashlet about this great victory. The daughter-in-law set me right.

"That was not such a great victory!" she said, laughing.

I refrained from asking how she knew. Eventually I learned. One late afternoon, in the village, I met Pfarrer Schnur's sister, a tall, thin, severe-looking lady.

"Come to the house and share our evening meal," she said.

This sounded like an order more than an invitation. I smiled and obeyed.

After a spartan meal, Pfarrer Schnur turned on the radio. Very low. A jammed emission came on. The BBC, I guessed.

"If they catch us," the priest said quietly, "it's heads off, you know that, don't you?"

Yes, I knew.

"For me, it would not matter much," he went on, "I am too tall. But you . . . you will be too short."

When the transmission was over, Pfarrer Schnur explained that he had to do the listening because the few farmers who possessed a radio were unable to make out more than a few words.

The next day, some selected villagers would learn that the Luftwaffe had been wiped out.

X L V

❦

now thawed. Our clear, gurgling mountain stream, within a
week, had turned into a muddy torrent that, mostly at night—
or so it seemed—gave out a long, low thundering.

One afternoon, it came close to overflowing its banks. Frau Döhnker
and her daughter departed. Emma and her father came to tell me that
there was a bed for me in Emma's room and a place for my animals in
their stable.

Then, Emma's father told me once more how one dismal spring
night, this "river" had destroyed the grist mill that had been right here
on this bare place where we were now standing. He had been a young
lad then, but he remembered. He had come down at dawn with his father. By then, the "river" had quieted down, but the mill was in ruins.
He had picked up pieces of the big paddle wheel, and downstream he
had seen the miller's calf, dead, still tied to a chunk of its trough. Oh, it
had been bad.

But, I argued, the catastrophe had happened, he himself had told
me, because thieves had cut down trees somewhere upstream and sent
logs floating down. The logs had piled up at some point, formed a dam
that had burst.

"Only the part of the grist mill directly by the water was destroyed,"

I said. "The old house with its meter thick-walls is still there. No one in the miller's family perished. Well, of course I don't want my animals to drown!"

"If you want to stay down there," Emma's father finally said, "you'll have to keep watch. The 'river' is going to crest by midnight. I know that 'river,' I have been watching it for more than fifty years."

"I'll keep watch," I said.

"If, at midnight, the water goes over that old rock there," he pointed at a large rock protruding over the stream bank, "you come to us with your animals."

"Yes," I promised, "I will."

I kept watch way past midnight.

It was eerie by the thundering stream at night. But I was so pleased with myself for not having given in to fear that I felt good and strong, and alert.

Curiously, the night was not very dark. I could save the candle of my old lantern. The raving waters, I fancied, gave out a light of their own. And I was not alone. My cat was there, still as an image, sitting on a huge log the stream had abandoned ages ago, her eyes aglow, her fur a still spot of pale light.

The water never reached the big protruding rock. By midday the next day, it was already receding and soon it stopped thundering.

Frau Döhnker and her daughter returned. We exchanged polite greetings.

One sunny noonday, I opened the stable door wide and invited my animals to come out. They took a few cautious steps in the sun, then at once decided to follow me under the trees.

The soft, damp earth there breathed and smelled like an animal. Unknown green things lifted up layers of rotting brown leaves. Furry moss shone anew along the path and on the rumps of ancient, worn rocks. On trees, millions of buds, swollen and sticky, were ready to burst open. The goat greedily snatched at low branches to get at them. I too, ate leaf buds.

All around the haunted house, grass was sprouting, thick and dark green. It must have been growing under the snow to be so lush that early. It looked like such good, nourishing grass.

The goat would not touch it. The sheep ate it. Then, surely copying the goat, quit.

I had little hay left. No farmer had any to sell so late in the season. How was I going to feed these fussy animals?

Luckily, the goat one day stepped on the narrow, rickety plank bridge that spanned the brook and resolutely walked over it. Then, standing on the other side, she let out an urgent bleating. I hurried to join her. The sheep took one look at the bridge, plunged into the wild water, and swam across.

The goat, as if she knew where she was going, led the way up the south side of the ravine.

The trail, dark and steep on the north side, turned into a gravel road that went up the south side's gentler slope in long pleasant curves.

I knew this road. We had taken it once, Abel and I. It led, three kilometers or so farther, to Mumlingen, a village bigger and wealthier than Bergheim. We preferred, we had said, modest, self-contained Bergheim.

Goat and sheep began to graze about one-third of the way to Mumlingen. The forest there was young. Bushes and short grass by the roadside grew in the sun. They tasted much better, I finally understood, than the most beautiful grass growing in the shade.

From then on, my animals expected me to accompany them to their chosen grazing grounds. They would not go without me. One hour or so before noon, they called under the poet's-room window. The goat knocked on the entrance door. If this did not bring me out, she would climb a knoll in front of the house. All her hair standing on end, she would slowly inflate herself. I would see her—she knew I would see her—I would get concerned, thinking she was sick—she knew that too. I would run down the stairs, she would deflate, and we would be on our way.

She won every time.

The cat got into the habit of going up the road to Mumlingen with us on every nice day. There were many nice days during the spring of 1944, in the little corner of the world where I happened to be.

There were also happy surprises. In March, two sturdy new bicycles arrived for us at Bergheim railroad station. Abel's brother-in-law, the army officer, had procured them. A miraculous feat in those days.

Going to Bergheim became a pleasure. I did not mind pushing the heavy bike up the trail out of the ravine, I was becoming so strong.

I rode with happy-go-lucky Emma. We visited her relatives in neighboring villages and, quite often, jovial Frau Keller.

Then one day, Abel showed up. He had a story he could hardly wait to tell.

The German army, now occupying what was left of Italy, needed more soldiers, and was recruiting photographers, artists, writers employed by the OT. And training them on the spot too.

"Well, yes, I was recruited," Abel said quietly. "I couldn't be trained," he added and chuckled.

"There was this old adjutant—I think he was an adjutant—who took us, a dozen men my age, to a field, and started to bark orders: 'Run, jump, lie down, get up . . . run.' Well, I fell down on a patch of grass and stayed there. . . . 'Get up, run!' the adjutant screamed. Then, bending over me: *Bist du taub?* [Are you deaf?] 'I'm dead,' I said. 'It's war, you have to have some dead.' I don't think he heard me, the poor fellow had to keep up with his good recruits. . . . Gave up on me, I guess."

I shook my head in disbelief.

"Target practice was more lively! I did not know how to hold a gun . . . my shots went off in all directions. I scared everybody. They had to take the gun away from me."

"Oh but you won so many bottles of bad champagne at the fairs in Paris!" I exclaimed.

"Yes, yes," Abel said, "but that was in another life."

Forty years old, I thought, and as happy as a boy over the outcome of a prank.

"Will you be able to get away with that . . . for long?"

"No!" And he laughed.

He enjoyed the dangerous game.

I should have been worried, but Abel's glee was contagious. To cheer us up even more, he mimicked an interview—between the dethroned and reenthroned short Italian king, Vittorio Emmanuel, and Mussolini, the demoted then reinstated strutting *duce*.

The story, told in the earthy dialect of Württemberg with its childishly softened Germanic accents, was insanely funny. I got sick with laughter, the first and certainly the last time in my whole life.

We had seven happy days.

XLVI

❧

I was always trying to identify the Nazis among the villagers. I was
not good at it. I remember saying to Frau Dashlet once that the
party boss of the village was a Nazi.

"Oh, no, he is not a Nazi!" The shy farm woman spoke so loudly, I
believed her.

The mayor, the councillors, the secretaries, on occasion, wore the
party badge. This did not mean anything, I knew.

Once, at some official gathering, I heard them sing *Deutschland über
Alles*. Heartily enough, I observed.

But then, on Sundays in church, I heard the same people sing
hymns no less heartily.

The Germans love to sing in groups. And they do it well.

More than one long year had to pass, and the French troops had to
be one hundred kilometers away, before I knew who was a Nazi among
the officials of Bergheim.

I was becoming fond of this ancient village. I had even learned to
appreciate and admire the rather ugly stoves built into every dwelling.
All alike in shape, size, and color, these one-and a-half-cubic-meter

blocks of sleek ceramic were too square, too shiny, too green, and much too big for any room.

But they had endearing features. First was the high bench topped by a thick slab of black slate built along one side of the stove. A cozy, warm seat for visitors weary from a long walk in the cold, the man of the house, aching and chilled from working outdoors, the very old, and the very young.

These stoves were really ovens that stored heat, then radiated it for twelve hours. All they consumed in a day were two or three bundles of twigs less than half a meter in diameter that the farmers made between seasons when trimming their hedgerows and fruit trees.

Early every morning, the bundles were shoved into a small square opening in the kitchen wall and lighted. When they had burned completely, a small cast-iron door was tightly shut and there was enough quiet, regulated heat for kitchen, family room, and the bedrooms that opened into it.

Bread was baked every week in these stove-ovens. Every big, round loaf showed traces of pale gray ashes on its underside.

The primitive economy of this out-of-the-way village, where nobody got wealthy and nobody got penniless, was as admirable as its homely stoves.

Its soil, wrested from forest and mountain, was not a rich soil, and to enrich it there was only the manure from farm animals.

The sparse economy had evolved under the oppression of overlords and the dangers of war. The villagers had a long training in obeying orders—and disobeying them. They delivered the required quotas of milk, grain, meat, potato to whatever rapacious government was in place. They also knew how to trick inspectors who came to count pigs, calves, and chickens. They had underground caches that had been there for centuries, and bricked-in walls too, for food and schnapps and the statues of their saints.

This was perhaps how they had developed, over the centuries, a dogged, sly confidence in themselves and their fate that I envied.

XLVII

❦

In April 1944, one sunny day followed another sunny day. *Hitler Wetter* this had been called in the years 1940 and 1941, when German armies had marched from victory to victory accompanied by glorious weather.

In 1944 when we had *Hitler Wetter*, German cities got *Coventryziert*, one after the other.

News came that in Stuttgart, younger brother's wife had been killed in her own cellar by a bomb. A weak man was now without a strong wife, a boy of six without a mother.

One Sunday in mid-April, I went to mass. Pfarrer Schnur was not a great preacher, but he grew eloquent when he urged his flock to be generous toward the starving city dwellers, and again when he once more announced the end of the dark days.

Out in the noonday light, church bells pealing confidently in the blue overhead, women hurrying home to put the Sunday meal on the table, men lingering in sober, small groups, I knew I was an outsider in this timeless, peaceful, and incongruous picture.

I caught sight of Herr Dashlet. Formal in his dark Sunday clothes, he stood alone by the church portal. I walked toward him. He greeted me in a loud voice. He had missed me three Sundays in a row, he said. Then, through clenched teeth, he whispered: "Gestapo's after you." He pointed at the sky. "Is that not gorgeous weather?" he exclaimed, then in a whisper: "Denounced as spy."

I agreed, this indeed was gorgeous weather.

"The wife was telling me yesterday, you must come to the house for a Sunday meal—careful, they watch us."

I thanked Herr Dashlet, but today, I said, I had to take the goat up the hill, I had no hay left.

I walked home, an automaton unable to think or feel. Later on, in the woods with my animals, I recovered. I had been denounced as a spy? Absurd. Reassuringly absurd. But "they" were going to search. Must burn everything written. Not enough—when they search, they find something. Must keep them from searching. Must keep them from searching . . . how?

In the afternoon, I came up with a scheme. I would simply do what every German woman did at this time of the year: a spectacular spring cleaning—which I had always found idiotic—and moreover, I would get help, that is, a witness. They hated witnesses.

I hurried to my neighbors. Took the shortcut, a nearly erased path that zigzagged among bushes and small trees to the top of the cliff in back of the old mill.

Emma was not home. Her parents, still in their Sunday clothes, sat on straight-backed chairs in the kitchen, dozing off. They did not say whether they were surprised at my breathless request. They only looked at each other and quietly said, yes, sure, they would send Emma to help me. Yes, tomorrow morning, early, they promised.

I spent part of the night burning notebooks, letters, old poems, and every scrap of paper with my handwriting on it.

Emma arrived early, enthusiastic as usual over the task at hand. We pushed the furniture out of the poet's room onto the large landing by the attic, emptied all the drawers, hung bedding and clothes on ropes strung between trees in front of the house. Then, getting tired of carrying things down the stairs, I decided to throw some out the window. Emma loved it.

This was when we spotted a verdigris uniform and black boots coming down the trail.

"We are getting a visitor," Emma said gaily, and she went on throwing cushions out of the window. One landed at the feet of the policeman. He was not amused.

"Come down this minute. I want to talk to you."

We knew this was the police chief for the county. His office was fourteen kilometers away in Söffingen. A tall, thin man of thirty-five with a yellowish complexion, he had a heart disease, the villagers said.

"Won't enjoy climbing out of the *Schlucht*," I thought as I obeyed his order.

"*Grüss Gott*," I mumbled.

He only gestured for me to follow him. He walked toward the brook, sat on the big log close to the water, and gestured again for me to sit beside him.

He took a handwritten letter out of his briefcase and read from it.

"You have been denounced as a spy."

I pointed at the lonely landscape of mountains and trees around us.

"What's there to spy about?" I asked quietly. "And I never go anywhere."

As if on cue, goat and sheep appeared, trotting and bleating. My good friend Emma had opened the stable door.

"You are helping war prisoners escape to Switzerland."

"Never had the opportunity," I said. Which was true.

"You know the way to the border, don't you?"

"No, I don't." True also.

"You are making propaganda against the Third Reich."

This accusation was, I knew, very serious. My talks with the villagers could be considered propaganda against the Third Reich. Students in their twenties had been beheaded for this very crime.

"From now on, you are forbidden to leave the county without an authorization signed by me, forbidden to talk to anybody about the accusations against you. And every Thursday at ten o'clock, you will report to my office. See you on Thursday. *Heil* Hitler."

XLVIII

"What did he want?" Emma asked.

The young farm girl had neither fear of the police chief nor much respect for his person or function. To her, as her father said, a policeman was a fellow in uniform who did no useful work.

"What did he want?"

"Oh, somebody has denounced me as a spy," I said.

Emma giggled.

"I know what a spy is," she said, "somebody who gets shot for stealing secrets from a gun factory. Not a woman who lives at the bottom of this old *Schlucht* with a cat, a goat, and a sheep."

I did not tell Emma about the other accusations, they worried me too much. Anyway, I had been forbidden to talk about them.

On the following Thursday, I reported to the police in Söffingen. The police chief was sitting behind his desk in his small office. He drowned my *"Grüss Gott"* under his powerful *"Heil* Hitler" and indicated the only other chair.

He wanted—higher authorities wanted—to hear from me a full account of everything I had done since the day I had entered Germany in February 1939.

"Everything?"

"Everything."

This was, I would eventually learn, one of the schemes the police used in order to catch—or trip—the accused.

The ordeal lasted over six hours.

I no longer remember what I said or did not say to the police chief but I remember clearly what I thought as I bicycled home: I will never make it alone. The villagers, I knew, were powerless. Herr Dashlet had already done all he could do.

I feverishly wrote three letters explaining my plight and asking for urgent advice. One letter I addressed to M. K. in Berlin—he knew me only slightly—one to Dr. G. in Stuttgart, the editor who had helped me get books to translate, and one to Christine's husband, who, I thought, would do his utmost for me.

It was raining hard the morning I took my letters to the mailbox. I could weep all the way to Bergheim, and no one I met on the road would know it. I knew only too well that sending those three letters was not much better than throwing coins into a wishing well.

Abel showed up unexpectedly. He had snatched two days from hell, he said. Would not tell me how. He was nervous, had become suspicious of our ancient walls. We went into the woods to talk. He told me about a punishment inflicted upon OT workers—men of over forty-five—for neglect of some duties. They had been made to stand in a deep ditch, had been buried up to their necks, and left there in the full sun for hours. Some had died, of course.

"If that's what they do to their own people, imagine what they can do to the others."

"They," it seemed, were no longer the Nazis exclusively.

"I had to punch the face of some brute who was boasting about decapitating a Jewess with a shovel rather than waste a bullet!"

True or not—the brute had been drinking—Abel did not regret the fight that had ensued.

"If we had had any weapon, one of us would have been killed," he said coldly. "You know, many of us will have to die before it's all over."

He had more to tell, I knew, but then he did not.

"Let's go to our neighbors," he suddenly said. "I want to thank them for being so kind and helpful to you."

One precious day had passed and I had not said anything about my own predicament. The longer I waited, the more I felt that it would be best to say nothing. What could Abel do in just one day? Try to persuade the police of my innocence? Impossible and foolish. He might get arrested. Moreover, I knew he would guess—as I had—who my denouncer was and I was afraid he would obey one of his rash impulses. But mostly, I just could not bear the thought of his anguish at knowing me in danger and realizing he could not defend me.

It was still dark the early morning Abel departed.

"To know that you are safe in this blessed old mill means so much to me," he said.

Only a few days later, a telegram addressed to me was received by the owner of a tiny café-farm located halfway to Bergheim. The only telephone in operation for the village was there.

Mariele, the café owner's daughter, a shy girl so tall and thin she was always bending at the waist, brought me the telegram.

"I never saw such a long message. I surely hope everything will turn out all right for you," she said, blushing.

She hurried away.

The telegram, sent by Dr. G. in Stuttgart, instructed me of my rights, advised me to contact a lawyer, and urged me to communicate any new developments to him, Dr. G., by telegram.

Everybody in the village, I had no doubt, knew the contents of my unusual telegram even before I did. And everybody began to talk and ask questions. Exactly what the police did not want.

"I forbade you to talk about the accusations," the police chief thundered when I entered his office on the following Thursday.

"I did not talk. . . . I wrote."

I don't think he heard me.

"We have not done anything to you yet," he said.

He sounded a bit defensive, I thought.

I signed the usual form, and was gruffly dismissed.

I waited for answers to my other two letters. None came.

One early morning, the forest warden showed up at the mill's door in company with a young woman, his niece, he said. He also carried a large suitcase.

"She is afraid of bombs," he said. "We don't have room in our house for her"—a lie, I knew. "You have a spare room, you can take her."

In a flash, I understood who the forest warden really was. And also that I had to take in the watchdog he was imposing on me.

The girl was dull and selfish. She robbed me of my sad, lonely, dear evenings with my cat. She never thought of offering us any of the bacon, sausage, and butter she had brought with her. Neither I nor my cat begged from her either.

We endured her presence for six whole days. On the seventh night, a deafening roar echoed for endless seconds through the twisting gorge. An uncanny silence followed.

At dawn, I knew what had happened. An enormous chunk of rock had detached itself from the top of the cliff and, missing the old mill's roof by thirty meters or so, had come to rest, split into two pieces of about one ton each, at the end of the trail.

My watchdog packed up. Didn't ask for help. She dragged her suitcase up the trail and in no time was out of our malefic *Schlucht*.

I could hardly hide my mirth. Emma and her parents, who had known my dismay about the niece's presence, looked at me with a bit of awe, thinking, no doubt, that I enjoyed some heavenly protection. I very nearly thought so myself.

On that day, Emma and I did some gardening. I had rented from her father a small patch of land up on the plateau. It had rained and weeds had to be pulled out before they began to steal nourishment from the cabbage we had planted and the carrots, beans, and onions we had seeded. I marveled at the tender plants coming out of the hard, compact soil.

"You have got to pull out the weed's roots too," Emma said.

"Careful you are not pulling out carrot leaves," she warned later on.

I, ignorant of coaching Schwartz Wald soil into growing something to eat, obeyed Emma's orders and warnings as best as I could.

On the first Thursday of May, I reported to the police as usual.

"We are going to have lunch at my house. My wife is expecting us," the police chief said as if this were an ordinary occurrence.

And so I sat at the dining room table in the police chief's neat stone-and-brick house between the police chief and his wife. The conversation was a bit strained, almost dream-like. I accepted a glass of cider, refused a tiny glass of good, comforting Schwartz Wald schnapps.

When I left, the police chief's wife gave me a bunch of flowers from her garden and a piece of twine to tie it to my bicycle handlebars.

I bicycled straight to Pfarrer Schnur's house. Until then, I had avoided telling my whole story to anyone in the village. On that strange Thursday, I told everything to the priest, from the anonymous letter and the denunciations it contained to the miraculous rock that had

Mireille Marokvia

chased away the Gestapo's watchdog and the extraordinary invitation to lunch at the police chief's house.

"Policemen listen to the BBC," Pfarrer Schnur commented. "On the other hand, this could be a trick," he added. "He could want to gain your confidence, make you talk. Don't accept his schnapps! Don't accept schnapps from the forest ranger or from that old turncoat, the carpenter, either."

"Oh, the carpenter too? Who wrote the anonymous letter?"

"Not a villager," the priest said.

"No, not a villager," I said.

XLIX

The grocer, at last, came on furlough.

I saw him one day when I stopped by. He sat slumped on a chair in the back of his store, white-haired, his hands resting on his knees. He lifted one shaky hand to acknowledge my greeting when I came in but said nothing. Was this the man I had seen one year or so before? He had had unusually dark hair then.

"They sent him on furlough because he is too sick to work," his wife said. "He can't eat, he can't sleep. . . . How am I to make him well in just one month?"

What had happened to this man?

Less than a week passed and the whole village knew. The grocer had spoken in his sleep. His wife had gotten a terrible tale out of him.

I heard it all at the Dashlets'. Frau Dashlet tried to tell me but she was so upset she spoke in the old dialect and I could not understand her. Her daughter-in-law came to the rescue. It was a wall around a camp the grocer had been building, she said, and he had seen what was going on in that camp. People were brought in, young, old, children, busloads of them. To be killed. With poison gas. And then their bodies were burned in ovens. The ovens' chimneys smoked day and night . . . day and night and, sure enough, one day the grocer had told an SS guard: "If our soldiers in the field knew what's going on here, they would throw their guns away." As a punishment, the grocer had been made to work inside the camp. And that was when he had gotten so sick he could not work any longer. So he had been sent home and told to shut up if he did not want to end up in there too.

"Do you believe it?" Frau Dashlet's daughter-in-law was choking with anger. "Do you believe it? I believe it!"

I said nothing. I put my arm around Frau Dashlet's shoulders. Her sorrow was greater than her anger.

After the grocer's nightmarish revelations, a new gloom invaded the village, sat in every home day and night.

There was still the hope that these were nothing but the delusions of a sick man. Some clung to that hope.

But everyone had to go on with the unforgiving daily chores of caring for the small children, tending to the animals and to the fields. Life went on, as it always does, with one more burden to carry.

I too took refuge with my animals for solace. These were not my people who where committing one more horrible crime, I told myself, my people were among the victims. But still, I joined the villagers in the overflowing church on Sundays and wept with them.

L

＊＊＊

One of the rare evenings I came home late, I encountered, standing in the darkness, at the door of the old mill, the tall forest warden and the short, bloated carpenter. The forest warden carried a gun.

"What a surprise!" I exclaimed and laughed.

The carpenter mumbled about his emphysema.

"You should not be out in the *Schlucht* at night," I said.

"I have to take the measurements for that cabinet you want me to make," the carpenter grumbled.

Indeed, the cabinet I had ordered one year or so before and nearly forgotten.

The two men tramped up the stairs.

Frau Döhnker opened her living room door and greeted them as if they had been expected friends.

The carpenter took the cabinet measurements and the two men departed.

The forest warden had not said one word. Carrying a gun, I guessed, was enough.

Even if I was, at first, more amused than frightened, the ludicrous visit, I knew, was a warning. I told Emma's parents about it. They shook their heads and said nothing.

Emma had to visit one of her uncles who was a guard at the Swiss border. Her parents would permit her to go only if I accompanied her. I was only too happy to do so.

We set out early on the last Sunday of May.

At first we had to push our bicycles up and down the narrow, tricky path along the brook and through the water at the shallows as far as the grist mill from which I fetched flour every month. From then on, we rode our bicycles on a dirt road along the larger stream our mountain brook had just joined.

After ten kilometers or so we left the riverside for a narrower dirt road that led straight to the guard's house. Three stories tall, under a high roof of gray shingle, alone among sparse trees.

This had been a lonely road; except for the grist mill, we had not seen one other habitation and met no one.

Emma's aunt and uncle were older than I had expected. They thanked me profusely for having come with their niece, whom they had not seen in a long time.

We had a splendid Sunday meal. Venison, cranberry preserves, coffee—real coffee. Then schnapps was put on the table and the uncle told stories. Border stories. The one I remember best was about runaway prisoners of war crossing the border.

"They hide in bushes and watch our sentinels pacing the border. The sentinels walk face to face, always meet at the same spot, salute, and go on back to back. See . . . run, and you can make it! When I was their age . . . The Poles run fastest!" The uncle laughed about that.

"Uncle, how can you tell they are Poles?" Emma asked.

"Oh, raggedy, skinny . . ."

"Do many cross over here?" I wanted to know.

"We used to have many. No more. The forest wardens get one thousand marks apiece, dead or alive. . . ."

Nobody said anything for a while.

"Me, I like to shoot boars," the uncle said.

The first days of June 1944 were sunny and dry. Too dry. Emma and I had to fetch buckets of water from Frau Keller's well and carry them in a cart half a kilometer or so to my struggling vegetables.

In the afternoon, I bicycled to Bergheim for news. "The Americans are in Rome," Pfarrer Schnur said. "The Germans have withdrawn without a struggle. Rome is intact!" I too rejoiced. I had lived in that beautiful city.

It must have been on the 8th or the 9th of June that the police chief showed up. I was outdoors with my animals, ready to go up the mountain. The police chief's "Heil Hitler" was a bit subdued.

My insolent goat went up to him and nuzzled his briefcase. He took out a small snack, unwrapped it, and fed it to the goat.

He sat for a while on the log by the brook, observed that the new sharp-edged chunk of rock had missed our roof by very little.

Holding my purring cat in my arms, I said gaily: "Yes, and I could be dead!"

In late afternoon, I rode to Bergheim in quest of news again. The police chief's demeanor had told me something had happened.

Frau Dashlet's daughter-in-law greeted me at the door with one sentence I have not forgotten.

"Die Americanern haben das ganze Atlantic Küste überrumpelt!" ("The Americans have taken the whole Atlantic coast by surprise!")

Later on Pfarrer Schnur, smiling, told me, it was not the whole

After the Anglo-American invasion of June 6, 1944,
the police chief feeds his snack to my goat.

Atlantic coast that had been *"überrumpelt,"* but a respectable length of
the Normandy coast.

And once more, we knew, the war would soon be over.

Next, Pfarrer Schnur said the mass for the dead over an empty
coffin draped in the Nazi flag that had, at the head, a soldier's
helmet resting on a cross made of evergreen.

Mariele's seventeen-year-old brother had met a hero's death somewhere in the east.

And somewhere in the west, Frau Keller's son-in-law, a plain OT
worker, had been killed.

L I

❦

I was by myself quite often at the old mill. Frau Döhnker and her daughter did not like our primitive accommodations and frequently went to a nearby town that, so far, had not suffered any air raid.

One day that I was alone, I watched, with some surprise, three slim young men coming down the trail. I had not seen young men in civilian clothes in many years.

I shouted my usual "*Grüss Gott.*"

"*Grüss Gott,*" they answered, and asked for the road to Bergheim.

I pointed at the road they had come from.

Then they asked for a glass of water. The clear, gurgling waters of a mountain stream were rushing by.

"Do you like goat milk?" I asked.

Yes, they did. They no doubt had detected my foreign accent. I had detected theirs.

They sat on the big log by the water, drank goat milk, ate my mediocre goat cheese and the rough dark bread I had baked. That was all I had.

I chatted about the places one could go to from my lonesome abode. Switzerland, for example. Only thirteen kilometers away. The way to go there was very lonely. With a stick, I drew a map on a sandy patch at the water's edge.

I delighted in sharing my recently acquired knowledge. I even told about the Poles who could run faster than anyone else across the border.

The three young men thanked me for the food and were on their way.

"To Bergheim," they said.

"*Viel Glück!*" I said.

"*Viel Glück!*" they said.

They made it. I would have heard if they had not.

Thursday. Again lunch with the police chief and his wife. Sad lunch. There were houses reduced to rubble on a nearby street. For the first time, bombs had fallen on the insignificant little town.

But I had no pity in my heart; as I was leaving, I told the police chief about the three young men who had, a few days before, passed by and asked me for a glass of water.

"I wonder who they were?" I said.

"Three SS I had sent to test you."

"Too skinny for SS men," I said.

"I have told you to shut up before!" the police chief said angrily.

I bicycled away.

I went to Pfarrer Schnur and told him the story of the three SS.

"You are playing with fire," the priest said severely.

True. I was tired of being afraid and cautious. I needed the luxury of playing with fire. And anyway, the war would soon be over.

L I I

❧

July 1944. My mother-in-law came to spend the summer months with me. I gave her the poet's room. I slept in the piano's room and worked at my translations on the kitchen table. I received a new book to translate every time I mailed one translated. Also a few words of complaint because it was handwritten. Sorry, I did not possess a type-writer. Would the author-editor care to provide one? None ever came.

I had few scruples about my sloppy work. I was only afraid that through some freakish occurrence, my father would come across it. I had not thought of assuming a pseudonym, and my name appeared on the shabby publications.

I had, so far, not had the heart to tell my mother-in-law about the grocer's revelations. She heard all about them when we visited Frau Keller.

"Oh, I don't believe any of it," she said. "Our people would never do such things."

I did not try to convince her. As Frau Keller said, it was better that the old lady did not believe such bad things. A time comes in life when one becomes too fragile to take in more suffering.

Abel's mother in her early sixties

My mother-in-law was not disturbed by the police chief's visits. It was good, she thought, that he kept an eye on the lonely place. When I told her it was me that he was keeping an eye on because I had been denounced as a spy, she thought I was joking. And I was so lucky, she told me, to be sharing a house with such polite, nice ladies as Frau Döhnker and her daughter.

My mother-in-law had turned her back on a present-day reality that she could neither comprehend nor accept. Moreover, her own harrowing past haunted her. She wanted to tell me about it.

She was a good storyteller. I could never retrieve the pathos she put into the retelling of the woeful story of her life.

Born around 1870 in an arid mountain village, she had been the beautiful, virtuous, eighteen-year-old girl who was jilted by her fiancé. In shame and sorrow, she had left her village and gone to stay with an uncle in a faraway foreign country. There a foreigner fell in love with her. She did not return his love but married him anyway and proudly returned to her village with him. But the young husband, a gifted tailor, could not make a living in such a small place. A recently naturalized citizen who did not speak German well, he craved the acceptance of the dour mountaineers and foolishly treated them to food and drinks at the local *gasthaus*. Meanwhile, he fathered children.

The story ended up with a picture I had seen more than once in old books: a woman pulling a cart piled up with bedding and, following her, six skinny children.

There were many dramatic episodes in the long tale. One was the birth of the fifth child. "I was so desperate to feed my first four children, I prayed for the nine months I carried this one that I would give birth to a dead baby," she said. "And I did . . . I saw the purple little body that lay at the foot of the bed!" Her husband, coming into the bedroom at that moment, saw it too. He playfully tossed it up in the air, and Abel came down into his father's hands, screaming.

"Of all my children, he was the best, the most gifted, the most caring," my mother-in-law said.

After her sixth child, she had divorced the man who could not feed his children. Abel had never told me.

I never saw a photograph of my father-in-law. His daughters had cut out his image from snapshots and family portraits. All they told me—because I asked—was that he had been a tall man, with a red beard, who could draw well—mostly horses—and had gone to live with some woman right after his family left him. He had died. They did not know when or where.

The struggle to feed six children had been a bitter one. My mother-in-law ruefully spoke of having been forced to send seven-year-old

Abel and a slightly older sister to beg for food from the farmers. "It was at that time," she said, "that Abel started to stutter."

Yet the long hardship had not changed her. She had lost neither her dignity nor her kindness. She was always ready to share the little she now owned with someone poorer than she. She neither criticized nor complained and was never moody. She was still capable of laughing.

Whenever she felt faint, she would ask for a "crust of bread," chew on it slowly, and soon say, with a smile, that she felt "revived."

Less than seven years later, she would suffer the cruel death of the stomach-cancer victim.

L I I I

❧

In the middle of June, Germany hurled onto London "the secret weapon" that Frau Döhnker, the forest ranger, and the police chief had knowingly whispered about.

"Even if our secret weapon totally destroys London, it won't keep the Russians from taking Warsaw, or the Americans Paris. And Warsaw is five hundred kilometers away from Berlin," Pfarrer Schnur said.

Would the war be over before winter? One did not dare to ask any longer. Besides, I had a farmer's worries: war or no war, my animals would have to be fed. The spring had been dry: there would be no hay for sale in the fall.

At a short distance from the old mill, on the sunny side of the brook, was an old clearing where fine grass grew. I would make hay there. *Verboten?* Probably. But then, I picked up dead wood in the protected wilderness area. *Verboten* too.

My neighbor cut the grass with a scythe, and my mother-in-law taught me how to make good hay. The cut grass had to be fluffed and turned several times a day. Strenuous on a slope. Emma was too busy at this time of the year to help me.

As soon as the hay was dry, it had to be brought under cover. I did not quite know how I was going to do that. But then Abel came on furlough. Unexpectedly, as usual.

We made big bundles of hay that we carried on our heads on the narrow path along the brook and hauled up the stairs to the attic.

Then we had a few quiet, almost cheerful days.

Abel played the sonata dedicated to his mother that he had composed when he was twenty.

"Sounds perhaps a bit too much like Mozart," he said.

But his mother was very happy.

Abel was going to be forty-two on July 21, 1944.

Since the dismal July 21, 1936, when he had been thrown into jail by the Franco regime, Abel had considered the day of his birth inauspicious.

July 21, 1944, was going to be another inauspicious day.

My memory has kept only one image from that day: Abel and a gray-haired villager I hardly knew, sitting side by side at a bare table, in the village *gasthaus* that had been locked and deserted for over five years. Two men, alone and silent, tears running down their faces.

Hitler had just spoken on the radio, announcing to "his" people that he was alive and well, having miraculously survived an assassination attempt against him—a proof that he was needed to accomplish the task providence had imposed on him.

He had also promised revenge.

Shortly after, Abel left. He had not told me he had been recalled to Berlin.

L I V

✤

Abel wrote from Berlin, giving no return address. He did not know where he would be sent next. The newspapers announced that men from sixteen to sixty would be called to fight in defense of the Fatherland.

On July 31, the Russians reached the outskirts of Warsaw (Poland).

On August 4, the Americans entered Rennes (France).

On the 8th, they were in Florence (Italy).

On the 9th, they were in Le Mans (France), 150 kilometers from my parents' home.

On the 15th, they landed between Marseilles and Nice.

And on the 25th, French tanks entered Paris.

At about the same time, a hasty, happy note from Abel brought news that he was departing for Bolzano, Italy.

The anticipation of the end became feverish.

Meanwhile, I had to make life at the bottom of the ravine bearable for my mother-in-law. She was lonely, I knew. She could not enjoy my animals as I did; the goat was too unpredictable for her, the affectionate sheep too clumsy, and she did not trust cats.

Verona, Italy, 1944 (*watercolor*)

I often walked with her to Frau Keller's. While she was visiting, I would rush to pull weeds and loosen the soil around my cabbages, carrots, and onions. And often, I would bicycle to Bergheim for the exciting news of the day.

Every Thursday, I "visited" the police chief. He was morose and distracted these days, but hopeful. Like many Germans, he still counted on miraculous secret weapons to save his besieged country. As for me, I had a hard time taking my weekly reports seriously, as if

the war had ended the day French tanks rolled down the Champs
Élysées.

One afternoon, the police chief came down the trail with a briefcase
full of small containers labeled in English. He was suspicious of
these things, which had been taken out of an American airplane that had
landed in a field near Söffingen, and he wanted all the labels translated.

I did not know English well enough to be able to translate every
word, but I could tell that in the mysterious containers there was nothing but aspirin, vitamins, concentrated food rations, and chocolate.

Was the airplane damaged? And what had happened to the pilot? I
wanted to know.

"Well, the plane was not really damaged. As for the three airmen,
they were dead."

"Now, that is strange!" I exclaimed.

"And you know," the police chief confided, "these peasants were going
to bury them like dogs. I cut pine branches myself to cover the bodies."

"Strange," I said again.

I told Pfarrer Schnur about the three dead airmen who had landed
their undamaged airplane in a field near Söffingen.

He knew the story. He only shook his head, did not tell me what he
thought. He was worried, obsessed almost, about the revenge the
Nazis were taking on the plotters of the coup against Hitler, "the best
men we still had."

"The dangerous days are not over," he warned.

During the summer, I had had some insect bites that had turned
into nasty abscesses. One, on the middle finger of my left hand,
was looking very bad. I could tell by the red streak that went up my arm.

I bicycled to Bergheim one morning, took a train that led to the only close town that had a hospital.

The center of town had been recently bombed. City Hall, banks, stores were in ruins, the church steeple mutilated.

The hospital had no door, no windows, no roof. I walked into a hall open to the sky, met a nurse, a quiet old Catholic nun in her traditional ample blue clothes and immaculate starched wimple. She looked at my finger, said nothing, led me to some sort of operating room behind a green curtain, persuaded me to accept the whiff of ether I did not want. "The doctor has no time to be careful," she said.

I hardly saw the young doctor. He wore a white coat and told me to count backward in French, then in German to hasten the effect of the ether.

When I left, holding aloft my throbbing, bandaged finger, two soldiers on stretchers were being brought in. I had nothing to do but wander between mounds of rubble until my late-afternoon train. Why had this quiet town had to be destroyed? Its only claim to fame, as far as I knew, was that it was located at the source of the Danube.

I came to what had been the main public square. It had been cleaned up. A patched-up canvas tent was being erected in the middle of it. A fairly big tent too. A circus? Then I saw children from Bergheim, five of them. I went to talk to them. They had come to the circus on their day off from school, they told me. They had never seen a circus before.

We watched the tent being erected.

It turned out that the children did not have enough money to pay for their entrance. I paid for them.

This was a brave circus crew. The trapezists were all women. The horse riders were all women. The horses were skinny, the tiger too tame, the bear too old. The trapezists had to double as clowns.

It was difficult for me to understand how the timorous parents I knew could permit their children—the oldest was fourteen—to take the train to the circus in a town in ruins. But then, as a pragmatic mother told me, the town had been destroyed already, there was no need to throw more bombs on it. No doubt it was safe.

I knew better. Alas!

L V

In September 1944, newspapers and radio touted "our" new secret
weapon—more lethal, more devastating than the previous one—
that we were now using to batter London. Whispered news was
that the British had taken Brussels and Americans had crossed the
German border.

October. Time had come to harvest my crop. I had grown enough
cabbage, carrots, and onions to last me over the winter. As pleased with
myself as a self-sufficient wartime farmer could be, I borrowed a hand
cart from my neighbors and, one early morning, headed for the fields.

I was not prepared for what I encountered: a shamble of discarded
wilting leaves and cabbage stems sticking out of the ground. Every head
of cabbage had been chopped off, every carrot and onion pulled out
and carted away overnight.

People from the bombed cities were coming day and night in search
of food, I knew. Someone hungrier than I has food now, I tried to tell
myself. But I had toiled too hard to be generous that morning. I was
even more angry than dismayed. It was no longer easy to buy food from
the farmers. They had discovered that money was not worth much by
now, and they expected clothes, shoes, kitchen utensils in exchange for
their goods.

But maybe the war would be over by Christmas. Herr Dashlet's daughter-in-law predicted it would. The Americans had smashed four kilometers into the Siegfried line and the Russians were in Prussia already.

One day at nightfall, as I was milking the goat, my neighbors' Russian volunteer worker suddenly showed up at the stable door. He was holding two eggs in one hand and smiling. A mere boy of seventeen, as shy as a wild animal, he had been working for my neighbors for over one year and I had been able to speak to him only once. Why had he volunteered to work for the Germans? I had asked.

Narrow forehead and high cheekbones reddening, *"Angst,"* he had stammered.

"From the mistress," the boy was saying as he handed me the eggs. Then, without pausing: "Man's running away at night, a Pole . . ."

"Food?"

"No, no." Gesturing to emphasize his halting words, the boy communicated that the Pole had a wounded foot or leg and needed bandages.

"Yes, yes," I said.

The boy ran up the zigzagging back path.

I hurried to the house with my jar of milk. At the door, I met Frau Döhnker and her daughter. They were returning from a trip to town and were in high spirits. They had gone to their bank, they told me—destroyed like the rest of the city—but, would I believe it, there had been, under the rubble, a door that led to an underground bank! They had had access to their money as usual. Now, was that not wonderful, and amazing how everything was so well organized!

"Amazing," I agreed, then proceeded to explain that my mother goat had eaten wet grass and become sick. "I'll have to go down our creaky stairs tonight," I warned.

The two women did not care much about my sick goat.

First I brewed a pail of chamomile tea, the classic remedy for a bloated goat—and my alibi in case I encountered some inquiring person on my nightly errands. The forest warden had told me once he could not see a thing in the dark. Was it true?

Night fell. A quiet, dark night. Carrying my pail of tea and, concealed under my peasant skirt, a bundle consisting of my only vial of iodine and homemade bandages, I was on my way.

I waited for some time by the stable. But then, suddenly afraid I would miss the man or possibly frighten him, I ran a way along the brook and deposited my bundle in a dip in the path—a wounded Pole would know what to do with it. I ran back, visited with my animals for a while, returned my cumbersome alibi prop to the kitchen, and went to bed.

I woke up with a start at dawn. Had my bundle been picked up? I did not want the forest warden to find it. I put on some clothes, tiptoed down the stairs, grabbed my pail of tea on the way, carefully turned the big key in the old lock, opened the creaky door, and there, confronting me, was the forest warden with his gun.

"You scared me!" I exclaimed reproachfully.

He grinned and pointed at my pail. "What's that?"

"Chamomile tea. My goat's sick. Drank some last night . . ."

"Ah, you were out last night. You saw him."

"Who? I did not see anybody."

The first rays of sun were peering through the branches of the trees.

"And who walked here, and there?"

With the muzzle of his gun, the forest warden was pointing at dewy grass crushed under hurrying feet.

"I did, I guess."

"Oh, sure, and running too. And what's that?"

There were dark spots on blue flowers.

"A fox catches rabbits every night," I said.

The forest warden motioned for me to follow him. He examined every foot track, then took the path along the brook.

"Another rabbit," he said, pointing at large dark spots on pale green moss.

He brushed over them with the back of his hand.

My throat felt so tight it hurt.

"Look, I know that some guy is on his way, and he is wounded," the forest warden said, patting his gun.

"Blood's dry," he grumbled. "And this is no occupation for a man with varicose veins!" But he did not slow his pace.

We were coming closer to the dip in the path where I had left my bundle. The pounding of my heart was louder than the forest warden's heavy steps on the damp earth.

If my bundle was still there . . .

It was not.

Elation made me giddy.

"Look," I nearly shouted, "I have got to see after my goat."

I turned around and walked back.

"He is not going to shoot me, is he?" I thought.

One hour or so later, I saw the forest warden again. He was engaged in a lively conversation with Frau Döhnker's daughter.

I told them my goat was fully recovered.

Once more, I had a not-very-cheerful lunch with the police chief and his wife.

I complained about the loss of my crop. The police chief made light of the incident. He was not worried about me starving in Bergheim, he said. I had more friends there than I knew, he added in a curiously re-proachful tone.

"What I am worried about are the Russians," he said. "The Russians are already on German soil, did you know that? Ah, if only these *Engländers* could understand that the best, the only way to save us all would be to make friends with us, and then fight together against the Russians. Amazing how stubborn these *Engländers* are!"

"Amazing," I agreed.

LVI

❧

now fell early during the winter of 1944-1945. Overnight, on All Saints' Day, at the bottom of the winter-dark *Schlucht*, solemn evergreens, nasty rocks, gray roofs, and muddy trails got draped and carpeted in magic white.

In the early morning, at the sight of the feast, a forgotten child-like joy filled me. I remember wishing I could make music. Wistfully, I visited the silent piano and lit a fire in the little black stove.

A bit later, I went prancing in the snow in my skimpy homemade bathing suit and took my daily dip in the icy, bubbling waters of the brook. Showing off for my own benefit.

The snow was too fresh for skiing. Emma and I merrily trampled in it to Frau Kessler's warm house. My mother-in-law was now staying with Frau Kessler. We expected some scolding and plenty of pampering.

Irmgard brought the mail while we visited: a newspaper and a letter from Abel announcing his visit for Christmas. This sent me dreaming: the war would come to an end right when Abel would be here with us, and the long nightmare would vanish.

The newspaper proclaimed a great German victory that was sending the American invaders reeling. I refused to believe it, hurried to Bergheim for real news. Indeed, Pfarrer Schnur confirmed, the German counterattack had been quite successful. So far.

I clung to my dream.

Abel came. For a very short visit. He hurried to tell me what could not be safely put into a letter. A few months before, during his last stay in Berlin, he had learned of the urgent appeal I had sent to M. K. when I had been denounced to the Gestapo. M. K., vastly exceeding his powers, had, first by phone and then by mail—on letterhead and with seals "borrowed" from the war ministry—ordered the police chief of Söffingen to leave me alone.

"Still," Abel warned, "the Nazis will not go down without dragging some of us into the pit with them, so be careful."

Another story Abel could not write about was how he had, against all expectations, been sent back to Italy. Stuck for weeks in a military camp near Berlin with older men processed for military service, he had one evening, on an impulse, given a painting, apparently to the right officer and at the right moment. Two days later he had been on his way to Italy.

Ah, the guardian angel!

Once more, we had to part.

"Stay right here," Abel said. "Wait for me. I'll come back. Someday."

We both knew it would not be soon.

Right after Abel's departure, the great German offensive faltered. Fifty thousand German soldiers surrendered, the BBC said. The American advance resumed.

Nevertheless, this would be a very long winter. Too much snow fell in December. My animals were safe and snug in a stable protected by

Dolomite Alps, Italy, *1944 (watercolor)*

cushions of snow. I dug a path to them often and never failed to feed them at the right time.

My purring companion stayed with me in the poet's room or nestled in the hay in the attic.

But in the forest that surrounded us, their food buried under the snow, the deer starved. All along the brook were many dark places in the snow marked by a circle of discolored hair, a grisly aura where a fawn had come down to the brook to drink and, too weak to climb back or escape, had provided a feast for fox, owl, rat, and boar. Not one bone was ever left.

. . .

There was by now little to report for the newspapers besides the heroic deeds of the Japanese who sank American warships by suicide bombings, and the crimes of the Russian invaders.

I missed some of my Thursday appointments because of the snow. The police chief did not reprimand me.

He had, I guessed, like many Germans, secretly begun to pray for a prompt American victory.

LVII

Around the middle of January 1945, I became unreasonably restless. At a time when every realistic individual was trying to crawl into a hole and hide, I craved to get out into the open. Or perhaps I simply wanted to get out of Bergheim because I was forbidden to.

I had to have a good reason to get permission from the police to leave the village. In a Germany attacked from all sides, her cities reduced to rubble, her armies cut to pieces, yesteryear's rules still applied: women were, as ever, urged to produce babies. And this was what would inspire the outlandish scheme, as exhilarating as a prank, I would hit upon to procure myself a vacation of sorts.

The closest hospital was in Freiburg, but I remembered having heard of a doctor specialist in infertility at the university hospital of Tübingen.

I wrote to this doctor, received a prompt answer scheduling me for a stay at the hospital. I rushed to the police chief with the doctor's letter and immediately got written permission to leave Bergheim. I boarded goats and sheep with my neighbors, Emma promised to take care of my cat, and I was on my way.

Tübingen was about 150 kilometers away. It was pitch dark when I arrived. There was no snow on the ground to light up the night either.

I did not try to find the hospital in a darkened town I did not know but booked a room at a hotel close to the railroad station and went for dinner at the restaurant next to it.

I sat facing the revolving glass doors of the entrance, a lone customer in a semidark room that smelled of rutabaga.

A few minutes later, I looked up from my illusory meal to watch, profiled behind the glass pane, a man I at once recognized. He had been a student at the boys' college of Chartres at the time I had been a student at the girls' college there. We had vaguely flirted. Seventeen years of our youth had passed.

He too had recognized me. He sat at my table facing me.

"You still have your beautiful hair," he said. "What are you doing here?"

"You still have the same enigmatic pale face," I said. "What are you doing here?"

We talked until we were asked to leave when the restaurant closed.

He had been a chemistry professor in a Parisian college when the war started, an officer in the French army, and a prisoner of war in a German camp for three long years. Boredom and depression had led him to consent to work in a laboratory in exchange for restricted freedom. He was even having an affair with the daughter of a prominent local Nazi, he boasted.

I wanted to know what kind of work he was doing at the laboratory.

"Watching flies misbehaving in glass jars, mostly," he said.

When we parted, one of us—I don't remember who—suggested a possible location for our next date: a Russian salt mine, perhaps.

A few days before this unlikely meeting, the Russian army had reached the Oder some fifty kilometers away from Berlin's suburbs and sent the German army into full retreat.

. . .

I very nearly enjoyed my odd vacation. It was longer than expected because I had my period when I entered the hospital and no tests could be made for one week.

I had a pleasant, clean, silent room to myself and a treasure on my night table: a leather-bound, oversized Bible in Luther's magnificent translation.

The nurses, placid, unsmiling, and efficient, belonged to a Protestant order. I liked them.

The fertility tests were done under anesthesia, and even if I had to get up, groggy and unwilling, and walk to the elevator because of an air raid, the whole experience was not unpleasant.

The proceedings, during the frequent day and night air raids, were conducted with silent efficiency. I will never forget the evacuation of the newborn babies down to the cellar shelter. Six of them would be neatly tucked into one big oval wicker basket that two strong nurses carried to the elevator. It was the only time I saw the shadow of a smile on the nurses' faces.

One Sunday morning, I attended the religious service. It took place in a large auditorium and was conducted by a middle-aged woman in black street clothes. Her reading from the Bible was fine. But when she asked for the Lord's protection of "our *Führer*" and exhorted us all to pray for him, I got somewhat sick and walked out.

Pfarrer Schnur, I remembered with some nostalgia, never felt obligated to make even the semblance of such a gesture.

I was sent home with a certification of fertility.

For some reason, I boarded a night train. I took an odd pleasure at being carried in the bowels of this shadow-serpent of a train that slithered through a land trying to be invisible, pausing briefly at ghostly railroad stations, hardly daring to whistle.

I had to spend cold, dark hours in a lonely, drafty railroad station waiting for a connection, and got to hear, from another stranded passenger, some of the dismal local news. Freiburg had been badly bombed, the hospital destroyed. Patients, their bodies ripped open, still alive, amputees had been found crawling away. . . .

I thought of the nurses calmly carrying their baskets full of babies. Did they know about the last news? Of course they knew.

LVIII

꘡

March 1945. Back to my bucolic haven. Snow melted away. Farmers worked their fields. It took two or three weeks for Abel's letters to reach me. In his last letter he wrote:"Berlin does not answer any longer. What does it mean?" Did the OT still exist? He did not say.

The newspapers reported little about the Italian front, the BBC nothing at all. Abel's mother lamented that the whole world had turned against us. True. She would never understand why.

"The end is near," Pfarrer Schnur said."But expect a last mad gesture from the dying monster."

The war was raging on faraway seas. We cared only about the war that was closing in upon us.

One clear, quiet April morning, two airplanes dropped bombs around Bergheim's tiny railroad station, never touching it but making big craters in the fields nearby and sending all the red tiles flying from the roofs of new workers' houses at the bottom of the hill.

By afternoon, children and old men had retrieved the tiles scattered in the fields, scrubbed them, and the women were putting them back on the roofs.

One late afternoon, as the shadows descended into the *Schlucht*, an endless straggly column of soldiers came down the trail, filed by the old mill, walked, one by one, over the plank bridge, and went up the path toward Mumlingen. All of them were young. Many had flowers tucked into the muzzles of their guns and giggling girls on their arms. The picture does not seem quite real even today. I remember only too well the rumbling, singing, iron-and-flesh war machine I had watched in 1941 as it returned from trampling over France.

A week or so passed. The sounds of battle echoed briefly through the ravine, then some villagers came down the trail. Somewhere, by the grist mill, a convoy of army supplies had been bombed, they said. There would be bread, and things. . . . I went with them.

We hurried along the brook, came to the grist mill. It was quietly churning away. A bit farther along the dirt road where I had bicycled with Emma when we visited her uncle, the border guard, we found antiaircraft guns still pointed at the sky, supply wagons, some over-turned, and horses grazing by the riverside. No trace of soldiers.

One of the supply wagons was a replica of the one my grandfather had driven to deliver groceries to farmers when I had been a small child.

There was no bread, nothing edible left. I scooped up some buttons scattered among pine needles and picked up a spool of bad thread. I spoke French to a black mare—she looked up. I patted her neck. A bullet had made a neat hole in one of her ears, another had grazed her rump. I fingered the part of the halter still hanging from her neck. I could tell she would follow me. A French horse, I said, and led her away.

I eventually boarded her with Herr Dashlet, rode her bareback. I could never find a saddle.

L I X

On the last Thursday of April, a beautiful day, I bicycled to the police as I had been obligated to do for over a very long year. Riding through Bergheim, I met Pfarrer Schnur and told him where I was going.

"The French are one hundred kilometers away," he said quietly.

"Well, a good-bye visit, then." And I rode on.

There was no one in the greening fields or patches of forest along the road, and no one on the streets of Söffingen. As if the land had been abandoned.

When he saw me at the door of his office, the police chief, instead of an energetic "*Heil Hitler,*" said in an even tone: "The French are one hundred kilometers away."

A fierce fire was roaring in his wood-burning stove. I did not comment on the beautiful warm spring day.

I had a modest, quiet, and—as we all knew—last lunch with the police chief and his wife. We had barely finished our ersatz coffee when the police chief got up from the table.

"Goebbels is going to speak. You want to hear him, I am sure," he said, addressing me.

He took a tall, slim bottle of schnapps and two tiny glasses from the cupboard, placed them on the coffee table in the living room beside a large radio set, indicated a chair for me, and sat on the other side of the coffee table facing me.

Goebbels spoke.

He must have spoken for quite a while because by the time he made his final prophecy, namely, the arrival of the four apocalyptic horses and their hellish gallop over the doomed soil of Europe, the bottle of schnapps was half empty.

The police chief gulped down the contents of his tiny glass, I, lady-like, sipped mine. Did he remember, I wondered, that I used to refuse his schnapps?

"That's it," the police chief said, stretching his shiny black boots and slapping his green-uniformed thigh. He turned off the radio. Somber music stopped abruptly.

I mumbled some appreciation of Goebbels's eloquence. I had heard only the thunderous end of the speech.

"Who is this man you know in Berlin?" the police chief suddenly asked.

This drew me out of my pleasant torpor.

"I don't know many men in Berlin," I said. "There was this artist who . . ."

"No, not an artist."

"Well, his brother was not an artist . . . he too had married a Jewish girl, a tiny woman, smaller than I . . . he would hide her at the top of a closet when . . ."

"You know somebody at the War Ministry," the police chief growled.

He was pacing the floor now.

"The War Ministry? . . . Ah, I remember, there was this officer we met . . . pleasant young man . . . killed himself, we heard. Maybe he was employed at the War Ministry."

"Look here," the police chief said. "Look here, when we had that investigation by the Gestapo about you, I got a phone call, then a letter from the War Ministry in Berlin, both ordering me to leave you alone. . . . Who is he?"

"He must have signed the letter."

"I could not decipher the signature."

"May I see this letter?"

The police chief ignored my question. He sat down.

"Oh, you have friends," he said. "Irmgard, the girl who carries the mail in Bergheim, she is the daughter of the party leader, you know. Well, when I ordered her to hand me all the mail addressed to you, she flatly refused. She told me that when she had taken the position of mail carrier, she had sworn never to hand the mail addressed to a person to anyone else. . . . I could not believe my ears!"

I said nothing.

"I could have forced her, you know. . . . I did not. You know what I did instead? I complimented her father for having such a fine daughter. Yes, that's what I did."

Because you had received a call from the War Ministry, I thought, and smiled.

Then the police chief once more told me how he had cut evergreen branches to cover the bodies of the three dead airmen.

"These peasants would have buried them like dogs," he told me again, and he got more agitated about the incident than ever before.

Shadows were filling the living room. The schnapps bottle was nearly empty. I got to my feet.

"It is getting dark and my goat has not been milked," I said.

"Well," the police chief said as he opened the door for me, "the French will be here in three days."

"When I was twenty-five, I could walk forty-five kilometers a day," I said. "They could be here in two days."

. . .

On the road, I caught up with Mariele. We bicycled together for a while. I had always liked her. I related the best details of my long talk with the police chief. I laughed a lot. But then my drunken bicycle kept wheeling into Mariele's.

"We'd better walk, don't you think?" the shy girl said.

We walked.

By the time we reached Bergheim, the night had become quite dark and my head had cleared.

In Herr Dashlet's front yard, men stood around a barrel propped up on a hand cart.

"I'll stop at the Dashlets'," I told Mariele.

She said good-night and pedaled away.

I stood my bicycle against the kitchen garden fence. A man handed me a glass of wine.

"Before the French get it . . ." he said. "*Zum Wohl!*"

The wine had gone bad.

"*Zum Wohl,*" I said.

In the Dashlets' hall, the freshly scrubbed stairs were still wet. The daughter-in-law stood at the top of the stairs. Her blond hair, perspiring face, and muscular arms glowed under the light of the single bulb hanging over her head.

She shouted greetings, dipped a large rag into a bucket of water, wrung it lustily, and threw it on the floor as I reached the landing. It was the Nazi flag.

"Go in. Go in," she said.

The door opened before I knocked.

Herr Dashlet, freshly shaved and silent, gestured broadly, inviting me in.

A smudged Nazi flag was spread out on the floor; one had to step on it in order to enter the room.

In the large, semidark living room, men stood in silence, a dozen of them perhaps, the councillors and anyone who had an official function. Neither the forest warden nor the carpenter was there.

No one spoke, no one smiled, no one paid the least attention to me.

In the middle of the room, under the only lightbulb hanging from the ceiling, a man was seated on a high chair, a Nazi flag draped over his chest and shoulders, his face invisible under a thick layer of white foam.

The party boss was shaving him, using an old-fashioned razor and, with a flourish, wiping the long blade on the Nazi flag.

I stood watching. Stunned.

Frau Dashlet discreetly pulled me aside and led me to the table for the traditional smoked bacon. I needed it.

Later on, when I took my leave—silently—the short, chunky party boss was being shaved by a tall, skinny mayor brandishing the razor blade with accrued drama yet masterly control and seriousness.

The sober elders, I had no doubt, would go on, late into the night, about the silent business of desecration they had devised for their own particular satisfaction, as methodically and resolutely as they plowed their meager soil, made hay, planted potatoes.

L X

⁕

Mid-April 1945. Everyone, everything, it seemed, waited. Goats and sheep refused to leave the stable.

One afternoon, I had just stepped out of the house carrying a basket of hay when a shiny dark-green car came down from Mumlingen, splashed through the water at the shallows, managed to roll through thick grass, attempted to negotiate the steep trail toward Bergheim, could not, backed down, and came to a stop right in front of the old mill.

A handsome, healthy-looking officer stepped out and handed me a tin.

"Could you make a cup of tea?" he asked.

I took the tin. It was at that moment that I saw the golden SS on both lapels of his collar.

I ran up the stairs, gave tin and message to Frau Döhnker, and took refuge with my animals.

When I came back later, mother, daughter, and SS officer were sitting at a small table out in the sun, having tea. They invited me. I shook my head and went about my business of filling a bucket at the brook. A hapless skinny chauffeur was there, drinking water. I gave him an apple.

Later on, in the early dusk of the *Schlucht*, the SS officer and his chauffeur quietly vanished among the trees.

It was about one day later that the sounds of a nearby battle reached us. Then people came down from Mumlingen, the old and the disabled carried in farm carts, young mothers walking with babies in their arms. The SS, they said, had decided to defend Mumlingen. They had entrenched themselves in the houses, and the French were trying to dislodge them. Most villagers had fled and taken refuge in the woods with their cattle.

The haunted house filled up, from the former saloon where the Döhnkers had stored unopened big crates to the attic where I kept my hay. Two bedridden old women stayed in the poet's room, wounded soldiers in the piano room. I unrolled my sleeping bag in the hall by the poet's room. At night, the whole place turned into a vast dormitory.

Orderly, quiet, undemanding, the refugees organized their new lives as best as they could. They had brought food, cows, and hay. They cooked in my kitchen and fed my animals as they fed their own. We all ate, somehow.

No one spoke much. We all listened to the fracas of their homes being demolished.

I don't remember how many days this lasted. But around noon one day, there was a lull. Every face lit up. The women called me for a special noonday meal, a steak. I had not seen one in perhaps seven years.

I entered the kitchen. There were a dozen people there, sitting or standing, two women by the kitchen stove, one soldier, both legs amputated, by the window. All waited to see me eat my steak, a reward for having opened my doors to them. And there, on my rickety round table, was the steak on a white plate.

I pulled up a chair. Loud shooting broke out as if the battle for Mumlingen had come down into the *Schlucht*.

Everybody froze.

Frau Döhnker burst in, disheveled, tremulous. I saw only the awful throbbing in the goiter.

"The French, the French are coming down the trail . . . shooting." She clawed at my arm.

"So I hear." I stepped away.

Then I saw, I felt, all those eyes riveted on me. Odd what that did to me, coupled with the deadly racket at the door. I ran down the stairs, threw the front door open, waved my arms, shouted something in French, or thought I did. My throat felt awfully tight. The shooting stopped.

I saw a white bed sheet coming down from the poet's-room window.

Three soldiers in khaki uniforms were approaching.

"Don't ever do that again! I nearly killed you," the officer angrily shouted. He pointed at a bullet hole in the door frame three centimeters or so above my head.

"Right thing," he said pointing at the white sheet.

He spoke perfect French. But he wore a khaki uniform.

"You are not wearing a French uniform," I said. I was remembering the "*bleu* horizon" of an earlier war.

"American uniform! And I am a Pole, and an officer in the French army," the officer said laughing.

He had splendid teeth, a ruddy complexion, and a strong, compact build. The young soldiers under his orders were two slim, pale Parisians.

"We saw German soldiers near this automobile. They ran behind the house. Where did they go?" the officer asked.

"They could not get into the house from this side," I said. "There is a path up the cliff back there."

"Where? Show us."

We walked to where the zigzagging path started.

A volley of bullets greeted us.

The officer pushed me flat down into the bushes. Now he was barking orders in German.

A gaunt soldier in a verdigris uniform threw down his gun and came toward the officer, his arms up. Other verdigris uniforms were fleeing uphill among the greenery.

We walked back.

"We are going to search the house. If we find any German soldier hiding in there, we will shoot you," the officer told me.

They searched the whole house, scaring everybody. They bayoneted my hay, found two German soldiers: one had no legs; the other, lying on a mattress in the piano room, had a broken back.

"Do these count?" I asked.

"No," the officer said gruffly.

When we were out of the house in the bright sun again, the Polish-French officer in American khaki grabbed me by the waist and kissed me.

"I knew you were one of us," he said.

"Oh, yes . . . and you nearly killed me!"

"*C'est la guerre!*" he said gaily.

Then my liberators emptied their pistols into the SS car and climbed the trail with their German prisoner.

LXI

Did I ever eat that steak? I don't know.

But I was praised and pampered as a savior, I remember. For weeks I got more eggs, butter, and sausage than the cat and I could possibly consume.

Frau Döhnker lost no time in assuring me that her daughter "would have done it too."

"Oh, sure, that was nothing," I said.

I visited the bedridden women in the poet's room and praised them for having used their brains better than I had used mine. Oh, no, no, they said, you are so brave.

We put back onto their bed the sheet they had displayed and fashioned a small white flag that the men fastened to the poet's window.

Word came that the battle for Mumlingen had ended. The French had won, then they had gone away.

Except for the young mothers and their babies, young, old, and disabled doggedly went back to their ruined homes.

Silence returned. So did my orange cat.

The mother goat stepped out of her stable, sniffed the air, and retreated.

Two or perhaps three quiet days passed.

Then, early one morning, a very anxious young mother who was sleeping in Frau Döhnker's back room came up to me. "SS soldiers got into the basement through a window last night. I watched them. And they lugged in heavy bundles and guns, many guns," she said.

There we were, half-a-dozen women, at the mercy of a few desperadoes bent on defending us the way they had defended Mumlingen. What were we going to do? Calling on the French for help would mean the destruction of the house. We had to persuade the men to leave peacefully. Ourselves, alone.

"Yes," the young mother said, " I will go with you."

We knocked gently on the former saloon's door. It opened a crack. Two eyes peered at us. The door opened enough to let me in, then slammed shut. Caught. I panicked. Not for long.

Three smallish young men in shabby civilian clothes were confronting me. Were these SS? Last-minute recruits, probably. Reluctant recruits, perhaps. And they had shed their uniforms.

I began to talk with some confidence.

I probably represented well how stupid, hopeless, and criminal the defense of this old house filled with women and babies would be. The men did not say one word, they stared at me out of eyes wild with fatigue and perhaps hunger. They let me out when I indicated I was finished. The following night, the young mother saw them slip out.

Then mothers and babies also abandoned my not-so-safe haven. I was left alone to get rid of the desperadoes' hoard. I wanted it out of the house at once.

It took me hours to carry out guns, two at a time, slung over my shoulders, and many kitchen aprons full of bullets. The hand grenades— I did not know what they were then—I handled gingerly. I threw everything into the brook from the top of the bridge.

Frau Döhnker scurried behind me.

"Ah, if my husband could see you . . . such good weapons," she lamented.

I glared at her.

I could see the gleam of metal down in the water from the bridge. The current, I knew, was not strong enough to flush away either guns or bullets. Silt, I hoped, would in time cover it all.

The next morning, the metallic gleam was gone. I threw a big rock down. It did not seem to hit anything solid.

I fancied Frau Döhnker and her daughter fishing all these good weapons out of the chilly water during the night. Did not quite know whether to be entertained by the image or worried.

L X I I

ꞏ❧❧ꞏ

May 1945. I stayed around the old mill for one day or two, waiting for whatever would happen next. One afternoon, I walked as far as Frau Kessler's home on the plateau. The only way we had to know about one another's fate was visiting.

Frau Kessler's grandchildren and Emma had come too. We all sat in the kitchen exchanging news. Nothing had happened in Bergheim. The French had come and gone. The worst, apparently, had been the noisy shooting at the bottom of the *Schlucht*.

Suddenly there was an odd thundering in the distance. We all rushed out, even my mother-in-law.

At the edge at the horizon, a short way from the village where I had bought my goat, two airplanes were throwing bombs at a tiny bridge.

A weird game. We watched mesmerized.

Suddenly the planes gave up and flew toward us. I tried to push our group back into the house. Nobody budged. One plane flew so low over our heads, we could see the pilot's face.

That must have been one of the very last days of the war. Soon after, I never knew how, but at once everybody knew, Hitler was dead and the war was over.

Just as soon, the rumor spread that the Americans and the Germans had together gone to war against the Russians.

I did not believe it.

On the next Sunday morning, I was on my way to Bergheim when, halfway up the trail, two French soldiers in khaki jumped out of the bushes and told me I was under arrest.

They escorted me to their commandant in Bergheim. During the three-kilometer walk we got to talk. A dozen soldiers had been posted around the ravine since dawn, they told me.

"What for? Just me?"

The soldiers would not say.

"You were observed going to the back of the house with a big basket and also filling up a bucket at the river," they said.

"I have two goats and a sheep," I said and laughed.

The young soldiers did not seem to believe me.

The commandant of a small garrison had been installed in the long-closed *gasthaus* at the village center.

Since I had been on my way to church, I carried a purse, and in it was the precious, never-used French passport that I had kept concealed for nearly seven years.

I presented it to the officer. I had married a German citizen six months before the war, I explained.

"There are many false passports," the young officer said quietly.

A card kept between the passport pages, fell out: the French consul's invitation to the Bastille Day celebrations of July 1939.

"Save that one. This is your best identification," the officer said.

During the next few months, I was arrested every time the garrison changed in Bergheim—it changed often—the old mill was searched and my hay bayoneted as often.

I was denounced again and again as a French woman living in this haunted house at the bottom of the *Schlucht* where she concealed SS.

The old village turncoat, yesterday's Gestapo agent who had kept an eye on me before, had now become the informer for the French.

But not every contact with my compatriots was unpleasant.

Once several officers of the Foreign Legion arrived in Bergheim. I happened to be there. They invited me to share their lunch.

I sat with some ten officers around a long table set in the newly re-opened airy dining room of the *gasthaus* where I had, less than one year before, watched Abel and another man sitting side by side in semidarkness, shedding tears over the failed attempt against Hitler.

I looked with some awe at the officers of the legendary Foreign Legion. In their thirties, all of different origins and backgrounds, all with different secrets in their past. Tough looking, tanned by the African sun, well mannered and handsome, and strangely alike. I tried to guess at their nationality. Impossible, they all spoke French very well.

The general conversation—banter really—developed about Hitler. Some officers thought he was still alive.

"And who cares?" one of them asked.

My gentlemanly neighbor suddenly banged on the table with his fist, making wine glasses dance.

"He is dead. I am telling you, he is dead, dead . . . dead!"

In his eyes was an icy blue fire I had seen before, the mark of the mad hatred of Hitler that some Germans harbored.

One afternoon, a strange automobile easily came down the trail and stopped right at the front door. Two high-ranking French officers stepped out and, with a smile, asked to visit the art gallery they had heard was housed in this ancient building.

They visited, looked at Abel's paintings on the walls. We had a long, pleasant talk. Then the smart automobile—an American jeep, I had learned—breezed up the steep trail.

Black Forest, 1945 (*ink*)

I was never arrested in Bergheim again.

The SS automobile too had gone up the trail, a week or so before, but in pieces and transported in a cart drawn by an ox.

L ife resumed, a bit more frugal than before.

Germany was now divided into four sectors respectively occupied by American, British, Russian, and French armies. The Black

Forest was in the French sector. Soon there was a French garrison in Sössingen, none in the small villages.

A few German soldiers returned, the sick ones mostly.

Frau Döhnker's youngest son had fallen somewhere in the east, her eldest son was jailed in the British sector.

French authorities required that every German adult carry an identification card in French.

I worked at the rickety City Hall typewriter to make out some two hundred cards.

Two good-looking, strong Russian girls begged me for German identification cards. I had asked them once why they had volunteered to work for the Germans. "House burnt, men dead, cattle stolen. No place to go," they had said. They did not want to ever go back to Russia, they told me. I made German identification cards for them.

Russian soldiers appeared in Bergheim a short time later. They had come to retrieve all the Russian "volunteer workers." They took with them my neighbors' Ukrainian boy and also a scrawny girl from Leningrad who had once told me that hunger had made her volunteer to work for the Germans. Both had been homesick. I doubted, even then, that they would ever see their homes again.

Enlarged photographs of the horrors recently discovered in the concentration camps were displayed at street corners. But there was something too abstract about the black-and-white posters. They failed to convey the intended message, I am sure. The grocer's revelations had had a stronger impact, coming from someone the people knew.

I confronted Frau Döhnker.

"Did you know about the concentration camps?" I asked.

"Oh, of course we knew! We visited Dachau. It was very clean."

"Clean?"

"Oh, you are so naïve!" she said.

Indeed, I was naïve, and getting frightened too.

Herr Döhnker came back. He was polite, avoided looking at people's faces, made himself quasi-invisible in his sober civilian clothes.

Frau Döhnker boasted how fast her husband had become the administrator of the war prisoner camp where he had been briefly interned. And there, it had been discovered that he had been born in Austria. He was an Austrian citizen! How convenient.

Summer had come. I made hay, without my mother-in-law's directions, and, alone, carried it to the attic. It turned out to be rather bad hay.

I made a vegetable garden in the space between house and brook. Backbreaking and useless.

I had forgotten the opinion expressed by my goat about the worth of vegetation that grew in the shadows of the ravine.

I planted raspberry bushes that grew tall and lush and gave oversized, pale, tasteless berries, and beans that produced abundant foliage and giant stringbeans not worth eating, they were so watery.

Toward the end of summer, the grocer came back. I did not see him but I heard that his hands did not shake any longer. He had walked for nearly six months, all the way through devastated Poland and

The author and the orange cat, spring 1946

Germany, to come home. He had recovered his good health. He also had gotten very angry right away. The dentist at Sössingen had refused to use the gold the grocer had brought with him to have his teeth fixed.

"This is not good gold," the dentist had said.

"Not good gold?" the grocer had ranted. "Not good gold? Those Jews had good gold in their teeth!"

What was the worst: the effrontery of Fran Döhnker or the "recovery" of the grocer?

The Dashlets' younger son came back. A changed man, his mother said sadly.

. . .

"Wait for me right here," Abel had said. Ages ago, or so it seemed.

The long-awaited last spring of the war and its cohort of surprises and dangers had come and gone. So had an endless summer. One late afternoon, as fall's cool shadows invaded the ravine, Abel walked across the narrow bridge that spanned the brook.

EPILOGUE

⬥❧⬥

One spring later, as we walked into Bergheim one quiet noonday, we came upon a singular display. A rug of Oriental splendor covered the whole width of the damp, dirt road and ran down the hill from the church portal to Main Street. Entirely made of flower petals and leaves, it told, we guessed, the life of Christ in pictures—no, paintings, beautiful, naïve paintings.

Who, among the men and women who worked the avaricious soil I knew, would have the time, the skill, or the strength for such an overnight accomplishment?

A lone woman walked by.

"Please tell us who made this?" I begged.

"Oh, *alle . . . alle.*" She hurried away, unwilling to talk.

Alle? Everybody? Had the grocer, perhaps, in the gray dawn, picked thousands of dandelions to make the golden aureoles for the saints' heads . . . Gestapo agents gathered daisies for the wings of angels?

We wanted to study every image. But bells tolled. Out of the church came men and women—no children—in a solemn, dark, silent procession. At the head, Pfarrer Schnur, erect, estranged, his face as white as his unadorned, starched surplice—the same one he wore to say mass over the empty coffins of dead soldiers.

Grim and resolute, priest, farmers, housewives came down the hill, their heels trampling into dust the sumptuous offering their hands and hearts had created.

An offering more precious for being kept secret. No one ever consented to tell us its meaning or reason.

I was deeply moved.

Not Abel. Nothing would ever reconcile him with the country of his birth. As more of the Nazis' dirty secrets were revealed, he got more desperate to get away from everything German.

We had to leave the haunted house; Abel could not bear to see the Döhnkers every day. I wept with Emma when we left. We spent one winter at Dashlets', then rented a lonely house on top of a hill in another, larger village. We boarded the animals with a farmer there, and I undertook the proceedings for our return to France.

I had to go several times to Baden-Baden, about 150 kilometers away. The French military government was located there.

The train trip itself was an adventure. A bridge over a deep ravine having been destroyed, the train would come to a stop at the edge of the ravine. The hapless passengers, after a perilous descent and a steep climb, would, sometimes, find another train waiting on the other side. Sometimes.

Baden-Baden had not been bombed much. It had been a renowned resort in the past, but now all of its hotels, restaurants, and most private residences were reserved exclusively for the members of the different armies of occupation.

I had no right to any of it.

German accommodations, if there were any, must have been well concealed. I never found them. There was, I recall fondly, one hotel reserved for Americans where I often got tea, toast, and jelly at five

The Kings of Württemberg Chateau, Stuttgart, 1946 (oil)

o'clock. Once a German secretary let me sleep on a narrow sofa in her tiny apartment.

Life was surging among the ruins. There was even less food than before. Once, I remember, I made a coat for a farmer's four-year-old daughter. I provided wool cloth, lining, a bit of fur. Got one four-pound loaf of bread for it. But old publishers were reviving, new ones were born. Abel got orders for book illustrations. A show of his paintings in Stuttgart was a near sellout. A publisher had bought a book of short stories I had written while waiting for Abel's return, and I had signed a contract for three more books. Abel was offered a teaching position. He turned it down.

In the middle of winter in 1946, I obtained a two-week French visa for Abel and me. We found Paris gray, sad, and cold. The apartments were still unheated. Abel visited the friends from the happy days.

"Why didn't you kill Hitler?" they asked.

"You were a German spy," they said.

"You were an officer in the German army."

Finally they said: "Listen, there are enough artists in Paris. . . . We don't want you to come back."

One of the friends wiped a tear when he said good-bye.

We visited my parents. During the German occupation, my father, as City Hall's secretary, had "procured" rations for the young men active in the resistance and sheltered them in his home. My mother and my father had aged greatly. They said that if we wanted to come back, they would do all they could to help us.

The friends of my school days welcomed us with open arms. They did not ask why we had not killed Hitler. But they advised us to be patient and wait a while, perhaps, before returning to traumatized France.

Back at the solitary, comfortable mountain house—it too possessed a classical green ceramic stove—we got a heartwarming welcome from the orange cat. I was grateful for everything I found again: cat, trees, earth, silence, even our spartan diet.

By then, news and letters from the people with whom we had shared suffering and hope for many long years were finding their way to us. Our faithful friends from Hamburg, Hans W. and his wife, had watched the destruction of their beloved city and the burning of their charming house, but they were alive and well. Fisherman Schulz and his wife sent a snapshot of their first baby. They were still happily sharing their small house with Hilde and her daughter, they wrote. Christine, brave, righteous Christine, had concealed an elderly Jewish friend in her country house for the last year of the war. Shortly after the war ended, the notorious Nazi whom we had known as one of Hitler's first sixty companions—and to whom Christine had always refused to talk—had one night, starving and in rags, knocked on her door. She had handed him food and one of her husband's suits but not permitted him to cross her threshold. The rumor was that shortly afterward, the resourceful rascal had presented himself to the French military and shouted: "Shoot me, I am a Nazi!" The bravado had served him well so far. Our lawyer friend in Stuttgart had become Vizedirector des Landespolizei für Würtemberg, which delighted us and did not surprise us. We had always thought that this man could not be just an obscure, angry little lawyer. M. K. at the last minute had been inducted to fight for the defense of Berlin against the Russians. He had miraculously survived and had recently married his fiancée. Many years later, M. K.'s wife visited us. No, she said, smiling, she had never heard about her husband's daring deeds on my behalf during the war. "He did that sort of thing for so many people," she added, "he probably does not even remember."

Not everyone had been lucky. The old farmer who had refused to rent us an apartment was now homeless. His village had been bombed, his farm destroyed. His whole family had survived and was now trying to rebuild. He humbly accepted the half kilogram of scarce nails that Abel brought him one day.

The police chief's wife showed up at our door once and begged me to write a letter to the French commandant on her husband's behalf. He had been jailed by the French. I did. After all, the police chief had been a sickly man doing a thankless job and, whatever his reasons had been, he had not been as nasty as he could have been.

We heard from our friends in Bergheim that the former "almost general" was now making a precarious living at doing for the farmers the demeaning jobs that they did not want to do. A piece of news that left us rather cold.

We had ties in this land. And life in a Germany without Nazis, even a Germany in shambles, would be quite bearable, I thought.

But hardly a few short weeks had passed after our return when Abel suddenly said: "We are innocents. . . . Nobody, nothing can keep us from returning to France. Let's go back!"

Arguing would have been useless. Moreover, this was true: we were innocents.

My trips to Baden-Baden resumed.

One goat died, we bartered the other and the sheep for food.

Finally, in February 1947, grand piano and furniture were hauled out of the *Schlucht* and put on the train with destination, France. Eight years before, almost to the day, I had come to Germany for a six-month stay. Eight years.

We had made sure that Abel's mother would remain secure and fairly happy with Frau Keller. When we said good-bye, the elderly lady, dignified as ever, showed neither surprise nor dismay. She knew her son well, she told me. She wished us luck.

I entrusted my orange cat to the daughter of a farmer who needed a cat, and shed one more tear.

It had been decided that we were, at first, going to stay with my parents on the Riviera where they were spending the winter.

Everything went as planned. We soon found an affordable, pleasant apartment. My parents spent one spring month with us before returning to their home for the summer.

The Riviera was no longer the Riviera we had known. Sky and sea were as blue as ever, but a gray mood, like a bad memory, lingered over the everyday life.

In midsummer, an art gallery in Cannes showed a dozen of Abel's paintings. At the opening, visitors and prospective buyers were chased away by a group of men—among them a former Parisian acquaintance—shouting: "Out with the Germans!"

On the following night, a truck backed into the gallery's show window.

Shortly afterward, we went to the local police to have Abel's passport stamped—which had to be done every six months. The police confiscated the passport.

News came that my orange cat had died of a broken heart.

A letter from Abel's sister related that her husband, the army officer who had often been so helpful to us, had been jailed by the French. An error that would be corrected months later, but, at the time, an added anguish.

Then one day at dawn, two policemen in civilian clothes picked us up at our home and drove us to their headquarters in Nice.

We had been denounced as a "suspicious couple," we were briefly told. Separate interrogations—patterned on the Gestapo's—followed. Five hours for Abel, seven for me.

Finally, late in the night, we were shown the rather stupid denunciation signed—alas—by five of our friends from the happy days.

"Did they sign with blood, or with red wine?" Abel asked.

We were released.

Months later, after we had returned to Paris, we would learn that the secret police had investigated for several months in France and Germany to make sure that Abel had been neither a spy nor an officer in the German army, and I had not been a traitor in the service of the Nazis.

In Paris, Abel soon found freelance work for advertising agencies. We sold some of my jewels and the grand piano. I converted a tall pile of French francs into a small package of dollars. On a crowded bus, it was taken out of my purse by a pickpocket.

A few months before, at the time of the harassments on the Riviera, we had filed a request for emigration to the United States. We had little hope that it would be granted.

But suddenly, in November 1949, it was.

We packed dizzily, managed to sell a few paintings, and once more said our good-byes, I with a heavy heart. I did not leave old Europe with Abel's ease.

On December 23, 1949, ten minutes before midnight, the *Ile de France* docked at Pier 1 in New York.

Abel and I, apprehensive and skinny, set foot on American soil. He was close to fifty, I past forty. We possessed the rudiments of the English language we had learned in school, and one fifty-dollar bill.

Yet it took only one day or two, and we wondered whether Abel's Old World guardian angel had not been waiting for us on the shores of the New World.

The day after Christmas, Abel rushed to show a few samples of his work to the art directors of two magazines I had picked at random out of the telephone book. Both happened to be prominent magazines, both entrusted him with some art work, which he executed in record time on the rickety table in our cheap hotel room. Between Christmas and New Year's Day, Abel earned more than the sale of his excellent grand piano had brought only one short month before.

During the very first days of January, Abel again paid a visit to *Esquire* magazine's art director. The amiable gentleman had, only two days after we landed, answered Abel's naive "Give me a chance" with a smile and a freelance job.

"Not so soon!" the art director exclaimed when he again saw Abel, his thin European portfolio under his arm. Suddenly he added: "Here is a desk and a chair. Want to work here, with us?"

Of course Abel accepted the offer.

I had been about to take a maid's job. I rushed to Columbia University instead, and registered for classes in English for foreigners.

On the way to America, December 1949

In early spring, we moved into a small studio in Greenwich Village: 55 Morton Street. Fresh flowers in the lobby, an elevator, a roof garden where, for the first time in our lives, we caught sight of a hummingbird. Someone presented us with a precious Siamese kitten.

Were we really starting anew, as if our most productive years had not been spent, wasted on dodging blows and surviving one day at a time?

We were. We did more than survive in the New World—we lived as we chose. Of course there were dark days. But there were many more bright ones. Some dreams went by the wayside: Abel never bought another grand piano. But there were moments, unexpected, enjoyable, when, in spite of Abel's misgivings, I wrote children's stories and he illustrated them.

Painting, one of the many dreams of Abel's youth, would become the solace of his last years. It was on a day he had been painting a mural on our patio wall that death surprised him.

Will I be as favored?

Over half a century has passed since we crossed the ocean with the immigrants' light baggage—there were thirty well-mended holes in my best dress—and hearts heavy with anxiety. I still smile today, remembering how full of promises was the ray of sun that coddled a valiant little tree by our window the first morning we woke up in our own hard sofa bed from the Salvation Army, and how reassuring, healing, was the mighty purr of New York City at our door.

ACKNOWLEDGMENTS

My thanks go to Professor Kevin McIlvoy for convincing me that, after a nasty illness, I could still write, to Dr. John Minor for his confidence and support, to Frederick Ramey for being the persistent and pitiless editor he is, to Richard Larsen for bringing back to life images that time was about to erase, to my physician Dr. Ann S. Mercer for keeping me alive and well a bit longer.